A
Case
for
the Angels

BY GAVIN LAMBERT

A
Case
for
the Angels

Gavin Lambert

The Dial Press, Inc. New York

 1968

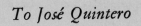

To José Quintero

DECEMBER 24th

THIS DAWN WAS AROUSED FROM SLEEP by a cry of brakes in the street, a door that slammed, an engine suddenly revved up and speeded away. At the same time, had been dreaming (*why?*) that I drove some kind of heavy truck or bus in the Sahara—professionally, that is for a living. So there's an area of confusion in what follows, a disputed frontier between reality and dream. Certainly I dozed off again. Woke. Rose at my usual hour of nine o'clock. Wandered in my usual nakedness from bedroom to living room, en route to kitchen, and saw at once that the day was extremely beautiful. Pausing, for I like to begin with a view, I glanced through my uncurtained, unblinded window.

On a canyon's rim, my house stands high above the Pacific. Gentle flight of steps takes me down to the street; beds that my own hands have planted make a border on each side, and a wooden gate—broken last week when Keith slammed it in a rage—droops half-open in front of Bellavista Lane. My car, 1963 Ghia convertible painted yellow and black like an enormous bumblebee, is parked immediately outside. Beyond it lies the world, into which I've decided not to go today. Prefer, instead, to remain within my modest compound, and to dwell, before making breakfast tea, on my Australian tea-plant. This pride of my beds, shrub some three feet tall with tiny bronze and green leaves, is garnished with crimson flowers no larger than a dime, curiously brilliant and unreal in texture, as if made by Mexicans from crinkled paper. Ocean fumes may cause the tea-plant to wither, or put out wretched and stingy little blossoms. Although three others have failed me in the past, this glorious survivor is my purest triumph, improbable but encouraging as another day blinks its eyelids open.

Noticing plenty of buds yet to unfold, I gave my tea-plant a nod of contentment and was gratified by so much promise and brightness in the warm winter sun. But in the same breath, lying on a step, just a few feet away, saw something Unspeakable.

No common scream issued from my throat. I became instead for a full minute exactly like what I saw. Inert, one paw in air as if rigidly protesting.

Next move was to the bathroom; slipped on white terry-cloth robe; opened front door; walked down steps to examine the surprise more closely. Bellavista Lane empty and quiet, except for myself and mortal remains. The Pacific a sheet of blue calm, so clear and solid it seemed to be slanting uphill, toward the sky. Then earth shook. Doors rattled. Glancing up, I saw a faint white trail disappearing, presumably, somewhere beyond the sound barrier. Thing, of course, never stirred. I walked back past suspended paw, stopped, realized I had to come to terms with it, and acknowledged out of nowhere, one dead dog. Not large, by the way; an uncommon breed, with pointed ears and foxlike head; stumpy tail, no longer than a sausage; and black as sin, night, hell and the ace of spades. After the shock, found myself privately naming it Deuce.

Both eyes blindly open, I remembered (re-entering kitchen), entrails and hindgut partially spilled out (filling kettle with water), some blood had originally drooled from mouth but now lay dry on the steps like hieroglyphic writing (switching on radio while waiting for water to boil). "Elusive Butterfly" came from my favorite station, which plays pop hits all day and night. When it finished, an announcer wished us Merry Christmas. My birthday falling on deathday of the year, I have to face—less than a week after celebrating His—the noiseless foot of time creeping up behind to whisper, _Mine_! Last year, remembered suddenly, I was thirty. This year shall admit to twenty-nine. My water boiled, and the announcer gave a newsflash. Young man standing on ledge of ninth floor room in downtown hotel for several hours had just agreed not to jump. Depressed because the army hadn't drafted him for active service in Vietnam, he'd been driven almost to suicide; life would lose all meaning, he felt, unless they let him do his duty. No word yet from Government on this. We'll be kept informed. Maybe, since it's Christmas tomorrow, he'll get his wish. "My Baby Needs Me."

Tea made, view from the window lured me back. Cup in hand, began to reconstruct crime stage by stage. (1) On morning of December twenty-fourth, while Dora Poley still slumbered in her lonely bed, motorist driving along Bellavista Lane in Santa Monica Canyon struck and killed a rare black dog. (2) Accident must have occurred immediately outside Poley residence. (3) Mr. Poley being away from home—correction, having walked out four days earlier—his wife was alone in the house with her Sahara dream. (4) Killer must have assumed that his victim lived at 167, so carried it through the open, broken front gate, laid it on steps and made his getaway.

Feeling cheered by this ability to reason calmly and sensibly, I then wondered: *will it hold up?* (1), (2) and (3) seemed watertight, but (4) contained more speculation than fact. Also, with a sinking heart, realized I'd never seen that dog before. In Bellavista Lane live one bassethound, one friendly bulldog and a nasty shrill little poodle. What was a strange, black, uncommon creature doing outside my house so early in the morning? Why the double coincidence of a motorist passing at the same moment? The cards of fate appeared oddly stacked—was Somebody up there marking the deck? Perhaps, after all, I knew the dog; tried to remember if I'd seen a small, sinister animal roaming around; felt certain I never had, but decided to go down the steps and check it out once more.

No shock of recognition followed. Instead, I noticed that it wore no collar or identification tag, and felt relieved. It began to seem much better that the dog and I were strangers, without name or associations to make a link between us. If we'd known each other, I'd have had to go to a neighbor's house on the day before Christmas with the news that a beloved pet had been killed and left on my property. A degree of suspicion would fall on me, and even if investigation proved I was telling the truth— MOTORIST CONFESSES!—the neighbor would always connect me with the death of Tigger or Lulu. Also, I don't greatly care for dogs. My sympathy for a loyal tail that wagged no more would lack the necessary passionate warmth. _"A heart of stone,"_ they'd whisper as I turned away, leaving them coldly stunned, _"Mrs. Poley certainly knows how to shut the gates of mercy."_

This feeling didn't last. Convinced again that an unknown murdered dog was the worst of all, would oblige me to deal with the officialdom of police, plead my innocence to an organization rather than a human being, like Kafka's K., I imagined the Law and a faceless delegation of pooch-lovers massed against me, saw glances narrowly exchanged as I repeated my story. They'd mark me down as a weird, disturbed woman, abandoned by her husband, who ran over a helpless dog and couldn't admit it. Actually dragged the body into her own garden to support a ridiculous statement that somebody left it there. _"Mrs. Poley? Santa Monica Police here. We've examined your testimony very carefully and have to ask you to return this afternoon for a polygraph test. You're entitled to refuse, but we'd like to point out that such a refusal speaks for itself. An innocent person, in the majority of cases——"_

Returned to house and sank, trembling, into a chair.

Leaflet under door. DOG–MURDERER! Anonymous phone call—"Hey there, Dora baby, run over any more good dogs lately?" WOMAN SETS FIRE TO HERSELF OUTSIDE WHITE HOUSE TO PROTEST!

Rising from chair, forced myself to make more tea. De-

cided to call Keith, assuming I knew where he would be.
Octavia answered the phone. She could tell from my voice
that something was wrong, and offered to come over immediately. "No, please give me Keith." Absolute silence.
Thought we'd been cut off. Footsteps, and he came on the
line. "Good morning, Keith. How are you? I hope I didn't
wake you, but——" and when I finished my tale, heard
another long silence; then a whisper; somebody laughing
(_not_ Octavia); and more footsteps. So the usual crowd
(pot, cheap wine, bedroom games, folk and rock) had
been there all night.

"A dead what?" Keith asked through a yawn.

"Oh God. How could you let me tell the whole thing
when you missed the most important word?"

"Once you start, you're not easy to stop." Voice quite
edgy, I thought.

"Dog. Dead black dog."

Another yawn, then, "It _would_ happen to _you_," and
Keith hung up.

On the phone again, I appeal to Chad.

Every unhappily married woman, in my opinion,
needs an attractive and sympathetic queen for a friend;
and Chad is instantly concerned, as reasonable as I could
hope for—ignore it, lay something over or around it, move
it, drench it with kerosene and set fire to it, bury it, dump
it from a moving car, call the police or a company that
hauls away trash—but becomes impatient when I refuse
all suggestions. Something, I realize, is holding me back.
Have no desire to suffer, dislike and resent this situation,

but can make no move until conscience, so to speak, lets me off the hook.

For I now believe that I believe we are no longer in the realm of the possible. As I see it, possibility demands the obvious. As *they* see it, possibility *is* the obvious—that ghastly unwelcome arrival outside my window, beside my lovely tea-plant. Common sense orders that it be removed very soon, for it's Indian summer this Christmas and after a few hours of sun the body may start to smell. So Chad wonders what stops me, calls me perverse, mad, wrong, depressing. I understand his impatience, sincerely wish I could see an honest way out of this dilemma, but feel it would be dangerous to rush into anything. Possibility, I repeat, demands the obvious, demands action—burn, hide, bury, complain, deny, pay someone else to do one's dirty work!— and the obvious is what I feel compelled, as usual, to reject.

"Chad, I'm prepared to state I feel this as deeply as I've felt anything in my life."

"All right, D.P., I'll come over."

Waiting for Chad, I'm on the phone again.

"Keith?"

He admits it.

"It's me."

Sigh.

"When I called you about that dog a little while ago, I forgot to ask if you're coming to our party tomorrow?"

"Sure. I told you I'd be there."

"Yes. You promised. It's very important to me to go

through this party together. After all, you invited everyone and never bothered to cancel. In my present mood,
with that dog outside, I couldn't possibly play hostess all
on my own. Can you understand?"

"I'll be there."

"Thank you."

"You're welcome."

"I'm not trying to make heavy weather out of anything,
but I'm really and truly deeply grateful."

"Try and get rid of that dog before the party, will you?
We don't need it. It's not festive."

"I'm certainly going to try. And Chad's going to help.
Together, I'm sure, we'll find a way."

He hangs up again. Obviously I shall never be able to
win with Keith. If I'm anxious, or jealous, or make a
scene, I fulfill his worst expectations. If I remain calm and
reasonable, he says: "God damn you." Being serious shows
my lack of humor. A joke proves that I don't care. There
seems no way out of this.

Anyway, forgetting dog for an instant, I wonder
exactly who and how many have been with him at that
house in the hills. A night with Jim and Andy Prell involves at least twenty—the young, dangerous brothers
themselves, of course; and Octavia I already know is there;
probably her friend Rosemary, whom Keith photographed
a couple of weeks ago; and Rosemary's (I understand)
regular playmate, who's called (I think) Mark; and a
dozen or so others, all attractive and pitiless, turning on,
dancing, vegetating, undressing around that huge, dark,
inadequately furnished mansion. While _I'm_ faced with a
dead animal outside my window, _they're_ waking up from

an orgy. They'll go back to it, what's more, without a thought for me.

Will he bring them *all* to the party tomorrow?

It's enough to make the angels weep.

Part of my problem, it seems to me, is that when I'm *truly alone* with it, as opposed to complaining about it on the telephone, I can't quite admit it's still there. Consciously I accept the truth, absurd or disagreeable though it may be; unconsciously I like to pretend that if I avert my eyes for a moment, make more tea or take a shower, it will have gone away by the time I look back.

Following this idea to its logical conclusion, I'm in real trouble. It means I hallucinate. Do I wish to believe *that*? No thank you. Reality, however grim (I've often said), is better than illusion, however gay. Then perhaps the reality outside means to test whether I mean what I say? Am I ready? What shall I do if I pass? So the arguments trap me in a vicious tormenting circle, and will be harder to break as the hours and shadows lengthen.

A long way away, whine of an ambulance. I see Cornish moors under a bleak, cold drizzle. Being a child I found personally quite hateful, so I've forgotten a good deal about it; but here's a memory always eager to come back. My father (Graham Parkhurst, M.A., a sweet, liberal, hopeless person) disliked remote control and felt one shouldn't go on living in London, getting one's eggs from Canada, one's apples from Australia, one's chestnuts from Italy, and so on. He moved my beautiful mother and me to a farm in Cornwall. After a year he'd lost most of his capital, and after another the War broke out. We hung on, growing turnips and potatoes. Paris fell. My mother failed to return from one of her long, secret walks. They found her dead on a beach, right below a cliff, about six miles from the farm. Official verdict was accidental causes. My father went on collecting the eggs every morning for a while, and writing his life of William Blake. He owned a book of pre-Raphaelite drawings, and the ladies who stared out from them, pale, fragile, a little melancholy, reminded me of my mother. Finally we returned to London and the bombs.

Nothing important, I believe, happened to me again until a late afternoon in October 1946. Eleven years old, I was a schoolgirl and moderately unpopular. (My classmates, inevitably, called me Dumb Dora. The nickname failed to wound because I knew I was clever, which was why they disliked me. My English teacher thought I showed imagination and affectionately referred to me as Parky.) This autumn afternoon, I'd left our apartment and taken a bus to Piccadilly, because Mrs. Neame arrived. Rather dowdy and much too apologetic, she was having a gentle affair with my father. They'd met, I believe, at some academic tea; her husband was professor of history at London University, and my father taught an English literature class there. One never knew when she was going to arrive, because it depended on Mr. Neame's visiting his sick mother, but one always knew when she'd left. At each visit she brought a bunch of violets and left them in my father's room. Their faint odor blended with that of old-fashioned central heating and whatever happened to be on the kitchen stove. This particular afternoon I was in my bedroom; heard my father open the front door and say, "Hello, Puss"; put on my dark blue hat and caught a bus.

Walking down Bond Street, I had the strangest feeling. This heart of elegance had been broken by the bombing, and the first thing I saw was an old woman with bandages underneath damp woolen stockings. She offered me, in a raw swollen hand, a measly bunch of roses. A pavement artist without legs or teeth squatted on his stumps and drew colored chalk portraits of our beloved Royal Family. A young street peddler with huge padded shoulders and an appallingly lecherous smile, approached me with a tray of matches, bootlaces, tiny unripened peaches. Out of a silver Bentley stumbled a couple of relics with walking-sticks and the dazed, bewildered look of survivors. None of this connected. Without knowing why, I felt a kind of panic. Later, I realized it was because I knew I'd never be able to deal with it, and hated things falling away, hated scars and break-up and mutilation and death. At fifteen I was certain that I couldn't, eventually, go on living in that city. I vowed never to fall in love there, never to commit myself to it. Fifteen years later, I received a proposal: not of marriage, but of serious cohabitation. (My suitor couldn't afford a divorce.) I'd lived for some time in the basement of a house in Hampstead, Victorian folly converted into separate apartments. In the old days, clearly, my quarters had been the servants'. For the princely sum of forty-five dollars a week I worked as part-time secretary to a theatrical producer, spending three days a week at his office, taking dictation, answering the phone, emptying ashtrays and returning plays. By now, in

the gray city, there was a touch of exoticism, turbaned In-
dians emerging from subways, American girls cruising the
National Gallery, Soho clubs advertising nudie films, out-
crop of Italian restaurants called the Villa Chianti or the
Trattoria Marinara. In the theater, the movies, in way of
clothes and life, my generation was said to be asserting
itself. I found much of this no more than provincial agit-
prop; atmosphere of general bedhopping struck me as
only the other side of the puritan coin. Not surprisingly,
my generation tended to ignore me. At twenty-six, I was
apparently a back number. I wore enthusiastically short
skirts and pale lips, punched my time-clock at the Villa
Chianti and new foreign films, but they felt I was only
trying to "pass."

Owen was a young poet who greatly admired Brecht.
This was by no means the only thing we didn't have in
common. He came from a working-class family in Wales,
demonstrated against the Bomb in Trafalgar Square, took
me to a club in Chelsea where one drank, argued and
listened to Tin Pan Alley. Our violent mutual attraction
was based on complete disapproval of each other. He felt
I was obstinate, snooty, swimming hopelessly against the
tide. I found him absurdly optimistic and boorish, accused
him of wasting his gifts through politicking, and refused
cohabitation as implying unconditional surrender to his
scene. About a month after this he abruptly informed me
he was going to live with someone else, and warned that
if I didn't take steps, I'd end up a bitter old maid.

Waiting for Chad, wonder how this dog problem will
affect our relationship; dislike the fact that, in his view, I

shall be cast in the traditional "feminine" role, pleading
for strong male help. He designs clothes, and although I
refuse to wear anything he creates, our feeling for each
other has always been warm and honest. Chad calls his
professional specialty "The Fragile Look," because he
wants to keep us girls feminine, and believes that Courrèges, Gernreich and their followers are basically hostile
to my sex. "They make women look like drag queens,
D.P. _I_ want them to look like women."

Naturally we argue about this. I point out that the drag
queen look is a simple expression of women nowadays
finding themselves in competition with men on almost
every level. Our clothes are bound to face up to this situation. Femininity becomes meaningless when society obliges
us girls to turn into half-men, encourages us to invade
such strongholds as politics, the army, bullfighting, the
police force, big business, and flying around the world solo
nonstop. In Israel we snipe at Arabs, in Ceylon we're
Prime Minister, in Russia we drive trains. A few of us have
even signed up for Space. "And look at _me_, Chad. You
can't honestly call me fragile, so why should I trick myself
up as if I were?"

Chad looks at me, admits the force of my argument
and regrets it; accuses me of making the worst of myself;
points out how at first glance, with my coppery hair,
startled eyes like a Siamese cat's, English bloom and
freckles, I appear extremely fine, delicate and correct; then
one notices unexpected strength to line of jaw, firm erect-
ness of head on shoulders. "Why can't you play it down,
D.P., instead of pointing it up? Take a leaf out of the
Queen of England's book." Am afraid I regard this as

trying to turn back the clock. Possibly we were happier in some ways before they forced us to seize power, but it's too late now to return to the nineteenth century. The male psyche is trying to keep up with moral problems of science, the female with new demands of virility. If we admit this and *cooperate*, we can help each other. I make a start by refusing to let them open doors for me. Also, I openly welcome the rise of people like Chad Weston, and not because it helps retard the population explosion. Who cares whether Spain is entitled to Gibraltar or China claims Formosa when erotic frontiers are breaking down? MAKE LOVE, NOT WAR sticks proudly on my bumper; also, GROPE FOR PEACE. Not long ago I thrilled a party by suggesting it was time for someone to write a grave sociological work entitled *The Heterosexual and Society*, in which a number of red-blooded males, who may remain anonymous if they wish, frankly discuss their problems and tensions.

Which brings me back to Keith. Sublimely ridiculous it seems that Chad, a dedicated but hopeless pimp, always introducing me to young men—"My dear, I think this one's for you" and afterward, "but you're *impossible* to please!"—accidentally brought us together. Almost a year ago he invited me to a poolside display of his new Fragile collection; feeling defiant, I arrived at the hotel in Beverly Hills wearing a Mondrian parka, white duck miniskirt and Courrèges boots. This, plus a hint of green eye-shadow, made it clear where I stood. It earned me pleasantly hostile or incredulous looks from the beaded bag, double-knit wool dress and turban-beret set. Sprawling on a chaise longue as far away from them as possible, but in full view, I accepted a vodka martini and stared through dark granny-glasses at the glittering pool shaped like a hot dog. Muzak snaked its way around palm trees and orange hibiscus, across sunlight and chatter. Then Chad, immaculate and tapered in seersucker, his face like an exhausted cherub's, appeared at the head of a chorus line of models, all in flowered linen and sickly crepe. The hard, unbreakable matrons whispered approval. Next month, I could tell, their lines would be more fragile and clinging than ever.

Camera in hand, Keith walked right past my chair, and a rough country boy stumbled upon the debutantes' picnic. I noticed his boots first of all, natural deerskin with collars of light fur, worn _outside_ a pair of chino pants. Scarlet shirt, tails hanging, was open at the neck. While Chad's eyes flickered with disapproval, Keith and I, never officially exchanging a glance, found ourselves on the same wavelength. The link established by our clothes was subversive and overwhelming. Ignoring the models, not even bothering to find them absurd, I concentrated on a shock of fawn-colored hair, a firm and narrow mouth, pale face and fiercely blue eyes; movements of a lithe, casual, buckaroo grace: expression at once remote and attentive as he checked the sun through a green filter. Palm trees, Muzak and matrons dissolved, I was driving alone from New York to Los Angeles through the endless plains of Nebraska, Kansas, Colorado, so mysterious and so boring— names of towns and rivers either romantically Indian (Pawnee, Cotopaxi, Chautauqua, Peru) or prosaically descriptive (Central City, Bluff, Higginsport), prairie alternating with freightyard, cowboy with plump little storekeeper, wildwood with main street. Rattle of ice cubes brought me back to Beverly Hills. As a white-coated Negro waiter poured me another martini, I saw the country boy walking toward me with his camera.

He aimed it without a word or a smile; I removed my granny-glasses; he clicked. After dinner that night, I strolled beside him through another disconnected landscape, the profoundly beautiful wasteland of Venice and Playa del Rey. Getting out of Keith's car, ruins of an imitation piazza confronted me, built years ago and abandoned when oil was struck nearby. Ragged bridge arched across nothing, pump moved automatically up and down, shacks crumbled in rows, new apartment buildings looked slummy and neglected before they were even finished, solitary palm tree drooped and sighed above a service station, ocean surf thudded in the distance. Turning a corner —past a used-furniture store with a blue Tiffany lamp, representing a wisteria tree, gleaming in the window—we walked down a short, silent street to his bungalow by the dunes. I glimpsed, beyond the living room window, a boat that his neighbor kept in his backyard. Keith went to the kitchen to fetch more wine; I kicked off my shoes; felt, because of the furniture, that I was in a motel; then poked around bookshelves containing a great deal of French erotica, and examined his photographs pinned to the walls. Most of these were high fashion, but there was one in color, larger than the rest, certainly not designed for _Vogue_ or _Harper's Bazaar_. Garlanded with pink feathers and smoking a cheroot, elderly Indian lady posed in ceremonial costume outside a tent.

"Malowaka."

Keith's voice startled me; hadn't heard him come back,

and turned to find him standing immediately behind me, barefoot, glasses and bottle in hand.

"And who, or what, is that"

"My grandmother."

"Is she for real, or an actress?"

"Hundred percent Ute, born in a wickiup."

"Some kind of a wicker basket?"

He nodded. "Turn a big one upside down and you have some kind of a house. Last summer I went back to the reservation to see her, told her to get out all her feathers. After I photographed her, we sat up half the night, arguing and getting drunk."

"Not still, surely, in a wickiup?"

"A tent."

"Not much of a step up, is it?"

He pinched my neck rather hard. "Malowaka quite rich now. She marry white man from Durango, he prospector, he strike gold." Bringing out an old photograph of her at twenty, he asked if it wasn't the most beautiful girl I'd ever seen. I admitted she was quite handsome. It was taken a few days after she married the prospector; when he died, she went back to the reservation, buying a little house that she stocked with five refrigerators, one gas and two electric stoves, some washing machines, a great deal of whisky. She seldom lived in it, however, preferring a tent that she pitched out front, in which she kept her TV.

"What did you argue about?"

"She despises the rest of my family and complains she's got no one to love or quarrel with. So she wants me to live with her." Keith sat me on his knees. "I've thought

19

about it sometimes. She's the only member of my family
I care about."

"What's wrong with the others?"

"When they quarrel, it's serious. About real things."
His nose twitched with distaste. "My father carried on
with other women and all that shit. Malowaka and I in-
sult each other just for the hell of it, then end up drunk
in each other's arms."

"I see."

"You're lying. But I wouldn't expect you to see. The
whole point is the morning after. Sitting outside, drinking coffee, looking at the mountains, laughing about what
we quarreled about. Beautiful! The others—I had uncles
and aunts and cousins, like everyone else, complaining
about each other for very good reasons, like everyone else
—would wake up with long faces in separate rooms. I
never understood living like that."

I looked from Keith's face, so candid and boyish as he
said this, to hers of the recent photograph. It was raddled
and flattish, eyes darkly slanted, nose like a small beak,
suggestion of grim humor hovering around the mouth.
The grandmother wore some kind of black tunic, and the
rest was feathers, fanlike spray of them above her head,
great wheel of them against her belly. Fierce eyes (Keith's
only obvious Indian inheritance) seemed to glare at me
because I sat on his knees. I suggested that we either switch
out the light or move to the bedroom. "I like both those
ideas," he said, and in what followed revealed passionate
invention as well as peculiar hostility. At the end of it all
he gave a nervous laugh and muttered, "Okay, that's it,"
before he fell asleep. For two or three hours I lay starkly

awake, wanting to move but unable to, his arm like a halter around my neck. I lit furtive cigarettes while he lay calm and still in another country, felt a twinge of melancholy that he could move so far away so quickly and effortlessly, and seem so contented there. When he stirred and mumbled, I turned to look at him, cricking my neck in order not to disturb his arm, remembering a book I'd recently read on the states and habits of sleep. He was emerging now, I could tell, from a phase that scientists call delta, deep and total and untroubled; drifting upward to the lighter, later, more active hours when pulse and breathing grow agitated, eyelids flicker with rapid movement as a world is entered beneath them. This world, I guessed from sighs and mumbles, had its quota of alarm. Wondering about it, I dropped into *mine*, remembering nothing when I awoke but suspecting it too of vague disturbances. Heard the sound of surf again; felt the weight of Keith's arm still across my neck; saw first his bare feet pointing toward the doorway open to the living room, then Ute grandmother in her feathers on the wall, then neighbor's boat beyond the window.

A moment later, Keith snorted and woke. His eyes raked my face, as if he stood gazing out from the deck of a ship, making me feel like the horizon—which was absurd, considering that we shared the same bed. Shoving me out with a remote, derisive smile, he ordered coffee, turned over on his stomach, pulled the sheet over his head. Oil pump shuttled up and down beyond the kitchen window. The view seemed just as confusing as that afternoon in Bond Street, but the difference was, this time I'd committed myself to it.

Another pinch on the neck startled me. Keith had padded silently into the kitchen, was staring at me with the same ironic, challenging smile. He lit a cigarette, coughed, spat into the sink. "Excuse me," he said. "Welcome to California."

Doorbell rings. I'm sitting on my lonely bed, Malowaka in her feathers, pinned to the wall, glaring across the room with steady, impenetrable eyes. I go to greet Chad, who stands at the top of the steps, elegant and twinkly in white linen trousers, pink shirt, paisley ascot, smoking a long brown cigarette through a TarGard filter. His pallor always astonishes me, not because it's excessive or unhealthy; but he stays out of the sun while dressing as if he always lived in it.

"Let me tell you something, D.P. It's a bitch."

"I couldn't agree more."

"I mean, you can't call it Deuce. That dog is—was—female."

"Then I rename it Octavia," I said and burst into tears.

He became, as I feared, immediately marvelous. Led me to couch, sat me down, put arm around my shoulder, refused to let me apologize. "I understand everything you're going through, so let's not discuss it. Let's just make up our minds what to do. Shall I call the police or the Humane Society first?"

Furiously grateful, I accepted his comfort in silence, let him pour me a brandy, stared out of the window. He told me to stop looking at it and swung me rather sharply around by the shoulders. "You're not to mope. I want you over this entire hump. Tell me what you'd like me to do."

"I'm sorry."

"*Don't* apologize. Tell me who to call."

"I can't discuss it now."

He looked at me, shrewd and mock-severe. "When people take an overdose of sleeping pills, you know, they can be saved if they *keep moving*."

"Do you happen to know, by the way, what kind of a dog it is?"

"Schipperke. Almost. Something went wrong, because it shouldn't have any tail at all."

"It reminds me of those creatures in Hieronymus Bosch. Weren't demons supposed in the Middle Ages to assume that kind of a shape, and possess nuns?"

"Now listen, Dora. We all love you——"

"*Who loves me?* Give me names!"

"Yours truly for openers."

"Oh yes." I laughed. "I love you too, Chad. You're the purest love of my life, I think."

He fitted another cigarette into his holder. "What a little puritan you are at heart, talking about purity because there's no question of sex between us." Then he sighed. Air of brisk authority vanished and he slumped down beside me. "But God knows, you may be right. God knows. I find it very sad."

"It's not possible." I was astonished. "You couldn't possibly be attracted to me. You once told me you found us all, from that point of view, the sink-holes of the world."

"I do. I was talking about the lack of connection, these days, between sex and love. Why do the young use sex as a weapon instead of an olive branch?"

23

"Tell me what happened."

"The usual story." Another, rather brave sigh. "Someone flagged me on the coast highway, night before last. He seemed so friendly and glorious and sweet. So *respectful*. I even wondered whether something might not, seriously, *develop*. When he turned really nasty later, I gave him all the cash I could find in the house. Practically a hundred dollars."

"Poor Chad." I put my arm around his shoulder. "I do wish you could find someone."

"I'm always finding someone. That's my trouble."

"You know what I mean. Permanent."

"My dear girl, should you be pushing marriage right now?"

"Oh God. Everything's too depressing."

Chad burst out laughing. "I'm supposed to cheer you up and straighten you out, D.P. And here we both are like Niobe, all tears."

Front door opened, apparently of its own accord. A black dog, on this side of the grave, bounded across the room, jumped on the couch and began licking my face. After the first shock, I recognized Octavia's terrier. The owner herself now arrived, tall and supple like Diana the Huntress, perfect oval of her face at its most severe, beautiful and predatory. "Radclyffe, get down from there!" she ordered, and the animal obeyed instantly. She bent over me, hands on my shoulders, scarlet lips slightly parted, eyelids blackened with kohl, rich chestnut hair tied in a bow at the back. "Since Keith refused to come over, I'm here myself. You poor angel."

Ironically gallant, Chad removed Octavia's right hand

from my shoulder and kissed it. "I told you, Dora. Everybody loves you."

"Thank you, Octavia. How sweet and thoughtful you are. And how hopeless it all is."

"What are you talking about, girl?"

"She won't agree to anything," Chad said. "She appears to be in shock."

"That's not true, I'm simply not ready for a decision yet. You see, Octavia, a straightforward extroverted person might well not give this whole thing a moment's thought, but _I'm_ prepared to state that I feel, as deeply as I've ever felt anything in my life, that I need time to see my whole way clear."

Octavia stared at me for a moment, then said, "You'll make me shit green, love, if you go on like that," walked over to the phone and dialed Information. Radclyffe followed, wagging her tail.

"Octavia, please wait a minute!"

She blew me a kiss, asked for the number of the local Humane Society and dialed it. "Good morning." Voice at its most alert and commanding. "And a Merry Christmas to you, dear, too. My name is Octavia Fell." (When she began modeling, Octavia decided to change her name, which had been Penelope something; the intersection of two streets in San Francisco inspired her.) "Somebody left a dead dog in the grounds of 167 Bellavista Lane this morning. Hit and run, I suppose. The owner of the house, Mrs. Dora Poley, is tremendously upset and has asked me to take complete charge. So will you come over and remove it, please, right away?"

After this, she listened impatiently for a while, answering only *yes* or *no*, then said: "It's completely ridiculous, but I'll do it." Hung up and walked back to me. "I'm afraid it's first of all a matter for the police."

"Oh God," I said faintly. "Why do we have to call them?"

"The Humane Society will not remove an unidentified animal unless the proper steps are taken to identify it first."

"There's no alternative?"

"None, my poor angel."

"Octavia, you shouldn't have *rushed in*. I feared something like this would happen. That's why I wanted to wait, and prepare myself for the great wheels of machinery starting to turn, the terrible official persons invading my privacy, asking questions, taking notes, hoping to trap me . . ." I got up, ran to the window and opened it; behind my back, I knew, Octavia and Chad exchanged glances. The uninvited, unclaimed, unnecessary thing seemed blacker and more rigid than ever. My tea-plant swayed in a light wind. A plume of white cloud waved briefly across the sun. Heard Chad say: "I told you before, D.P., *stop looking at it*." Ocean stretched away, clear and winter-blue. With a gasp, I noticed a child sitting on his bicycle, immediately outside the gate. Staring at dog, then at me, pitiless and accusing in his curiosity, he called out to ask if I did it.

I slammed the window shut. "My God, soon the whole street will know about this. I'm going to lie down."

Flopped on bed, I could hear them whispering on the other side of the door. Closing my eyes, I saw Keith stretched on another bed, relaxed and content after a night at Prell Hall. If he thought of me, which was improbable, the fact would be recorded by a brief, mocking smile or an indifferent shrug. Now Octavia was sitting on my bed, taking my hand, leaning her face very close to mine. I felt her breath on my cheek and was mildly disgusted with her for using this situation to try and make me again. (She succeeded once, at Prell Hall, which is one of the many grudges I bear that place.) "Now listen. Don't be an idiot." Spoke in a voice she considered thrillingly low. "You're not handling this right at all. You're making it much worse than it has to be."

"Octavia, I appreciate your wanting to help, but——"

"You want Keith to help. I know. That's your little scheme."

I turned my face away.

"And believe me, it's very unwise to try and _use_ that dead dog to get him back."

I tried to turn over on my stomach, but she wouldn't let me.

"You fool no one, my poor angel, pretending you're terrified of the police." Clearly, Octavia had decided upon her shock-treatment approach. "You're just playing helpless in order to feel helpless. And blame Keith for not helping you."

"It's hateful of him not to come. Doesn't he have a responsibility?"

"You know that's a word he never acknowledges. And if you took that line on the phone, you only confirmed his worst fears. Did you?"

"I don't know."

"Did you cling, Dora? Did you depend?"

I sat up indignantly. "I stated the facts. If one's left, all by oneself, to deal with something horrible like that, isn't it reasonable to give one's husband the facts? You know my views. A partnership between a man and a woman, or any pair of lovers, has to be equal and independent."

"I know your views, but you don't always carry them out." Octavia ran her forefinger across my cheek. "Oddly enough, Keith was talking about that last night."

"Oh. Thank you very much. Pulling me to pieces up in the hills, in front of everybody, were you?"

"No, my poor angel. Everybody loves you."

"Keith does *not* love me."

"I think he does. Or, I think he *might* . . ." Finger moved down to my chin. "It was simply that he brought up that little matter of the bullfight."

"Oh God. *That*. It was almost a year ago."

"He's never understood what made you lie to him."

"But why must he harp on a minor episode out of the past?"

Chad appeared, telling Octavia he'd like to speak to her. "And by the way, D.P., I had a good idea and went out after that child."

"In itself, that *can't* be a good idea. Haven't I made it clear to both of you I'm not ready to make *any* move yet?"

"I offered him a dollar if he could find the owner of the dog. If he succeeds, we can get rid of it right away. His name, in case he calls, is Greg."

"Good work." Octavia followed him out of the room. "I'd rather bet my money on a smart kid than a clunkhead cop."

Closed my eyes and sat beside Keith in his car. We were driving toward the Mexican border. Having still received no sign or word of affection on our first morning together, I felt silently peevish. Clouds above the Pacific moved slowly nearer land as my lover continued to talk about his grandmother. Just before we left the mail came, bringing a letter from her. It described in an almost illiterate scrawl how they'd begun drilling for oil on some property she'd bought, and enclosed a photograph of herself, standing ancient but proud beside a gleaming derrick.

To change the subject, I congratulated him on living in Venice. "I think it's marvelous there. Wish I'd thought of it myself, instead of renting a shack in Malibu, where one pays through the nose simply to live by the ocean."

A long, disinterested pause. "I don't understand anyone living right on the ocean. The surf gets on your nerves."

"Yes." Saw through the windshield a billboard advertising Sleep-Tite, pretty fair-haired girl with closed eyes and a vacant expression. "Keith, did you see a movie called _Repulsion_?"

"Jesus, no. Who wants to watch a girl going nuts for two hours because she's afraid of guys?"

I read the _Los Angeles Times_ for a while.

"So what's the matter? You're not talking. Like a Dexamil?"

"Thank you. I believe I might."

He indicated the glove compartment. I opened it and saw a pillbox beside a small plastic bag apparently full of dried weeds. Removing both, I swallowed Dexamil and

29

sniffed weeds; glanced at my driver's profile, fine and straight, and thought Keith was still in another country this morning, but on purpose. Nothing aggressive about his remoteness, yet beginning a conversation with him made me think of requesting an audience with the Pope.

"Keith. Is this marihuana?" He nodded. "Yours?" He nodded again and transferred it to a pocket. "You're going to take it across the border? Just like that?"

"Sure. Does it make you nervous?"

"A little."

"The Dexamil should fix that."

"I hope so. Do you smoke it often?"

Shrug.

"I've tried it only a couple of times, unfortunately in dark gloomy rooms with people assembled for the one grim purpose of getting high——"

A quick, amused, guarded stare. "You know the Prells? I've never seen you there."

"No. Who are they?"

"Brothers."

"Why did you think I knew them?"

"You might have been describing their place. Superficially."

"Well, I've never been there. But I find myself bristling with opposition to that kind of thing. I'd like to have my consciousness changed, or expanded, or whatever they call it—only for the time being, of course—but not in an atmosphere that seems part doctor's waiting room, part church and part flophouse."

"The Dexamil seems to be working."

It seemed obvious now that he was testing me. No one

who smokes pot leaves it in his car by accident; the little
sack was waiting for me to discover it. Everything, probably—coolness, sarcasm, perverse insistence on grandmother, whisking me off to Tijuana—was Keith's attempt
to find out how far he could go. There are people who
declare a war of nerves when they feel the beginning of an
involvement. I switched on the radio to my favorite station
and nodded to pop music until we reached the border.
. . . "By the time I get to Phoenix . . ."

As they waved us through (no trouble with the plastic
bag in Keith's pocket), the light had that somber brilliance preceding a storm. Under it, the wretched hillside
hovels looked more pitiful than ever, one expected only
pigs or dogs to emerge from them. Aficionados filed in
their cars through streets that looked like an open-air
movie set—suggestion of false fronts everywhere, in the
souvenir and duty-free liquor stores, the dives, the bureaus
for instant marriage and divorce, the extras representing
local poverty. Idiotically, I pretended to Keith that I'd
seen a bullfight before, wanting to surprise him because
he thought all English people were against them on account of obsession with kindness to animals. Worried for
a moment about my bluff being called, then thought: if
one has read Hemingway, it must be possible to tell a
cuadrilla from a picador.

Black clouds massed above the sunny side as we took
our seats in the shade of a box. Black bull scudded out,
pulled up immediately in front of scarlet cape. Keith stiff-
ened in exactly the same way, hands gripping the stone
ledge of the box, and I had an intuition of someone bred
from birth for hostilities and theatrics. Felt a wave of love

and fear; didn't dare speak to him, for he seemed alone and immersed in the spectacle, unaware of my presence; tried to concentrate, through the slit of our box, on the sullenly beautiful young man in a gaudy costume, who could neither read nor write but flirted brilliantly with death. He moved so close that I could see the sweat on his face and a scar across one hand. Gasps and *olés!* sounded unnaturally loud. Bull gored a horse and I leaped to my feet without knowing why. Aware that Keith noticed, I had to sit down again, feeling foolish and jittery.

Pink banderillas stuck in its neck, the bull stumbled slightly. We glanced from sky to arena as light went very dark. Delicate and perfect as a surgeon's incision, the killing sword struck the animal's neck; it stood very still, blood spilling down its haunches, then rolled over on its back to die. The young matador kissed his own palm and pressed it for a moment against his victim's forehead, embracing the wound with a gesture that seemed to combine love, triumph, pride and benediction. He bowed unsmilingly and the storm broke. In the pewterish sand, blood turned to a deep, hard, tragic red, silver and purple of the matador's costume became solemn mourning, and the rain —like a cloth laid over a parrot's cage—poured silence on the crowd. It dispersed as horses dragged the dead black creature away. From our sheltered side, Keith photographed it all, cool and impartial, just as I'd first noticed him with the fashion models by the pool in Beverly Hills, twenty-four hours ago.

A burst of thunder was followed by soggy trumpet music. I had to raise my voice against it. "KEITH!" He looked startled. "I'M TERRIBLY SORRY!" He looked puzzled. "I'M AFRAID I'M GOING TO BE SICK!" He looked annoyed. A woman jostled past, goring me in the ribs. Luckily, I had a handkerchief.

"When one considers the thing *I've* overlooked," I said as Octavia came back into the room, "what's so important about pretending I'd seen a bullfight before?"

She looked at me, lips slightly parted again; ravenous, but certain of (and a little sorry for) her prey. "He agreed it's nothing in itself, but said he could give me a dozen other instances that added up to something."

"It's not true. What?"

"Keith has his moments, you know." She was checking herself in a mirror now; turned right, turned left, found nothing out of order. "Like all instinctive people, he can be much too clever and acute. Dora thinks she's a modern woman, he said, cool and with it, carrying on about equality and freedom and all that shit. But she's really an old-fashioned bluestocking with an inferiority complex about men."

"Oh God. Do you have a cigarette?"

Octavia stuck one in my mouth, snapped out her lighter, bent over me. Then she lit one for herself, sat on the bed, pressed the palm of her hand lightly against my forehead. I remembered the young matador and his dead bull. "You're so warm, poor angel. Not feverish, are you?"

Bedroom door opened again. Chad announced that the police would be around shortly.

I stared at both of them. "How can this be? Who did it?" Then remembered Chad coming in earlier, wanting

33

to speak to Octavia alone; had been so preoccupied with Keith calling me a liar that it didn't occur to me to suspect them of plotting.

Chad ordered me quite sharply to feel grateful. "We've made up our minds not to let this sink you. I told you before, what are friends *for?*" He waved good-by, promised to call later. I wanted to beg him not to leave me alone in the house with Octavia, but felt too angry, proud and weak. Closing my eyes, I prayed for some wicked instinct to throw her offguard; thought immediately of Prell Hall; endured a twinge of pain but knew I was on the right track.

"How is Rosemary?"

Her composure dropped, like a thermometer when it's shaken, two or three degrees. "I'm a little worried about that girl."

"Why?"

Octavia moved to the window, stared at the bamboo jungle I'd planted outside to screen the view of and from 163's carport. (There was already a fence with horizontal slats; but I'd once observed Mrs. Arlene Cody, stockbroker's widow, right-winger, president of the Westside Toastmistress Club, peering through from the driver's seat of her 1959 Cadillac.) She kept her back to me, so I couldn't see her expression, but I noticed her hand tug nervously at the bow in her hair. "Believe it or not, we're getting to be more than a three-ring circus."

"There's someone else, apart from you and Mark?"

"Andy Prell." Blew out smoke. "He got in the act this morning."

"How?

"The three of *them* were taking a shower together."

"But what can that mean? Is Andy seriously interested in Mark?"

"No, only in Mark *and* Rosemary."

"Where does that leave *you*?"

Spiral of smoke drifted through the window, into the bamboo, like a question mark. "You know I'm not possessive. And incapable of jealousy. I'm only concerned about Rosemary going too far along *that* road."

"You're right, Octavia. Take it from me." Ill temper, which had prompted me to begin this conversation, ebbed completely away; sympathy and remorse rose to high tide. "I once told Keith I'd nothing against the act of infidelity itself, that's unrealistic and Victorian, but if your whole approach to the sexual act becomes just a search for kicks, you end up unable to relate to anyone." Saw her head nod in emphatic agreement. "You turn into a swinger, and swingers are terribly depressing, because they've chosen to escape from all personal feeling." Another nod, another trail of smoke. "I realized that when Keith tried to start this thing about not going to bed with me unless Jim Prell was there too, and I wouldn't, so he went up to the Hall almost every night all summer. Octavia, how I understand what you must be going through!"

A tear crept down my face. I stared at her proud firm back; admired it; wondered how she could keep it up. Then she stubbed out her cigarette, turned around, and I was astonished to see her smiling again.

"You're still not with it yet, Dora. They invited me in."

"To the shower? My God. Did you?"

"It was a difficult decision. Since I love Rosemary, I can

be attracted to Mark because Rosemary is. That's what they call viable." Grimace. "But physically, Andrew Prell —I know he's a handsome boy, and he's more interesting than Jim, but he turns me off."

"So you stayed out of it, after all?"

"And retired, mysterious with grief, to my room? A year ago I'd have probably done exactly that, but I'm learning." Octavia sat on the bed again. "I joined in, and ignored Andy. So pointedly, in fact, that he beat it."

"You're fantastic."

Octavia shrugged.

"You really are. I could never do a thing like that."

"You remained on the outside," said Octavia dryly, "looking in. No good, my poor angel. You lost him." Took my hand. "So why don't we leave them all to it? We're really much more right for each other, you and I, than——"

"*Please*. Not now. Not again. Besides, the police will be arriving."

"That's got nothing to do with it." She gripped my shoulders, then kissed me on the mouth. "You can't think of anyone but Keith, can you? Eh? Huh?"

"You're right, so please stop it." When she wedged her tongue between my lips, I bit it hard. She moved away to the window again, calmly presenting her splendid back.

"I'm sorry, Octavia."

"So am I, my dear."

"It's just no good." *How dare she make me apologize?* "I know it sounds dreary, but I'm not in the market right now."

"It *is* dreary."

"I can't help it." *The secret of her strength lies in making me feel abject. Wish I had it.* "I'm sorry."

"You could make up your mind, cut your losses, and see Keith for what he is."

"Tell me what he is."

"A beautiful enigma, with a very simple, ugly secret." She turned around, smiling hungrily again. "Keith lacks a heart. That's why he'll always prefer sensation to feeling. Since it's the other way around with you, you'll never work it out. In spite of my facade, I'm like you. I want feeling, too. That's why we'd be so good for each other." Stood over me. "To hell with them all. Let's go off somewhere." *Never gives up. I admire that, too.* "We could go to San Diego, I know everyone there."

"Did you notice who Keith was with last night?"

She turned away. "There's a car outside, must be the police. Would you like me to handle them?"

"Perhaps you could start them off. I'll join you in a minute."

She gave me a last, pitying look before closing the door. Remaining on bed, I went back to that endless, ominous Tijuana day; drank a couple of brandies in Caesar's Bar while the storm cleared and Keith refused all my excuses (overexcitement, lack of sleep, Dexamil, weather), insisting that my reaction to the bullfight was typically British, sentimental and female. We went out to the street, where a tout accosted us instantly. He offered his sister, his brother, anything we wanted, even the goats that Keith playfully claimed to like best of all; finally suggested an establishment in the mountains called The Palace of Vice. Beautiful, said Keith, we have to go, and soon our cab was bumping up a dirt-track road against the setting sun and silhouetted hills. We drew up outside a shack that looked like a canteen in an old Foreign Legion movie, reddish glimmer in one window and no other lights to be seen. I mentioned that it might be wise to keep the cab waiting. Keith promised the driver fifty pesos extra if he didn't go away, then opened a door, bowing me ceremoniously forward into a large bare room. It was filled with mariachi songs and dreadful whores. I reeled back from the sight of so many fat, greasy, tacky girls with paper flowers in their hair, smelling of stale perfume and beer. A string of red bulbs lit the room; trio of musicians made monotonously plaintive sounds in one corner; from another, the Madam waddled over and asked if we were interested in the moving pictures. "Three for five dollars, señor, one boy and two girls, two boys and one girl, three girls, three boys, or just one boy one girl, any combination you wish, three for five dollars." Forget what combination Keith wished, but he complained later they hadn't got his order right. Whores drifted contemptuously away, dismissing us as gringo voyeurs, and we sat on a couch in a cell-like room, white brick wall serving as projection screen. One boy one girl was the usual scene of interminable fellatio. Girl put on nun's habit at the end of it all. Keith seemed riveted, however, smile haunting his mouth while the Mexican projectionist behind him stood sleepy and impassive, probably stoned, forefinger caressing a grief-stricken mustache. The Madam dropped by to see that all was well, offered Keith his choice of girls, hinted to me that the projectionist was available; we said we had everything we needed and sent her packing. After one boy two girls, we left, whores smirking at Keith, sticking out tongues at me, music wailing. The cab was still there and we lurched away.

Because of the twisting road, solitary glimmer of light in the window vanished then reappeared. "I had a good time there," Keith said with a yawn and a stretch. I replied that I found it sad and ugly, received a quick stern look and was told I didn't understand. So beautiful, he explained, to be a stranger; opening that door, entering that room, you lived in a world that held out no hope or offer of human contact, were spared the everyday traffic of concern, affection, misunderstanding, pain; you bought a drink, a movie, the use of a body, arrived and departed without an obligation or a name.

"I'm not sure I find that so wonderful."

"Have you ever tried it?"

"What?"

After a pause, he said: "The point is, there's no sweat."

"But if that's what you want, where do *I* come in?"

Received no answer except his hand holding mine firmly for a moment, then a suggestion that we go back to Caesar's for another drink. Finding nothing but tourists there, whooping it up in South-of-the-Border hats, we walked around the corner to The Green Cat. Musicians blasted the dark and smoky air, silhouettes clustered around tables watched a stripper in high heels and bikini mincing up and down a stage. She looked bored and hostile. After fifteen minutes she ambled over to the piano, picked up a glass, drank, turned around, removed the bikini's upper half, shrugged, removed the lower, turned around again and presented her buttocks. "Okay, that's it," Keith said, taking my arm and guiding me out to the sound of bravos and thumping on tables.

The car was parked in a side street reeking of garbage. As Keith unlocked it, I heard a meow; saw a child squatting in a doorway, staring into the gutter, where a kitten lay, perhaps three weeks old. It screamed with rage rather than for help. No doubt it had been screaming half the day, desperate with complaint at being abandoned, being hungry, going to die, furious at the indifference of people walking past. Now, in the darkness, it had attracted only the hard, useless curiosity of a little barefoot girl in a dirty shawl.

Keith took my arm again. "Are you the kind that hangs around at street accidents?"

"No."

"Then leave it alone." His face was stony. "Get in the car."

"I know they have a different attitude toward animals —and toward death, for that matter—but can one just leave it there?"

"What else can one do?" He mocked my tone. "One can kill it, of course, if one likes."

"You can't be serious."

Keith smiled at me, then kissed me on the cheek. "If you try and take it back, they'll throw it out at the border. If you give it away to anyone here, they'll eat it." Opened the car door. "So be glad, when you see something like that, you're not responsible."

From dying kitten to dead dog, thought grimly, and not responsible for either; that's *our* story. Rose from bed and decided to face police. The living room was empty except for Radclyffe crouched on the windowsill, looking out. In that typically devoted, resigned, puzzled way that I find so maddening in dogs, she was staring at her mistress—herself sitting on the steps outside, staring at my black visitor. She was like someone in a Yoga position and I didn't want to disturb her, but she looked up for a moment and said, "False alarm. Just a neighbor's car pulling up in the street." Then withdrew again to another private silence, hooding her eyes.

"Octavia. Are you all right?"

"Yes." She patted the steps. I sat down at her side. "But this whole situation is starting to get through to me." An orange butterfly alighted briefly on dead dog's nose, then skittered away. "I'm finding it strange and odd," Octavia said. "I want you to know I understand the way you must have felt."

"Well, thank you. I'm still feeling it, by the way." It seemed wrong to enjoy the sun. Ocean, more solid than ever, still slanted toward the sky, pale and a little hazy now along the horizon. "But that's the first thing anyone's said that hasn't made me feel unspeakably neurotic. Did you know Chad actually compared me to a person who's taken an overdose of sleeping pills?"

"Pay no attention. He's a drama queen."

"To be fair, it was really to suggest that I must keep moving. But while I appreciate the need to take practical steps, I've got to pause first. I've got to absorb the *thing* itself."

"You're right. Completely right. I guess I'm doing that now."

Another butterfly, on the left ear this time; then, less agreeably, a fly on the creature's nose. It remained. I clapped my hands, and it buzzed off.

"Tell me," Octavia said, "what was your first thought, when you first saw it?"

"After the shock, I wanted very much to give it a name." A bluejay squawked from a telephone wire. "This may strike you as foolish, but it somehow made it a little cozier."

"You're right. Completely right."

"I called it Deuce. Because it was black and mysterious, and made me think of the devil."

"I called it George."

"When?"

"Just now, when I came out and found it wasn't the police. For some reason I couldn't take my eyes off it, so I sat down, lit a cigarette and decided it was George."

"But it's female."

"So it can't be Deuce, either."

"I know."

Another fly. Octavia beat the step with her hand. It flew.

"You mustn't be angry, darling, if I tell you that when Chad discovered it was a bitch, I renamed it. I named it after _you_."

She took my hand. "I'm not angry, just curious."

"Then I burst into tears."

"So I'm not a bitch after all?"

"You never were. Not really." Nineteen fifty-nine Cadillac emerged from the carport next door. Mrs. Cody, in a cheerful hat, was at the wheel. She gave us a deeply

interested glance, wished me Merry Christmas, and drove
away.

"Go on," Octavia said.

"I'm sorry. I'm wondering if that awful woman noticed the dog."

"Probably. But she was quite some distance away. I'd
guess she dismissed it as alive and belonging to me."

"What a marvelous thought."

"Go on, girl. You were saying I'm not really a bitch."

"Yes. What I meant was, when I first met you it was
like seeing that dog through the window this morning.
You dropped from the sky, too. You were the first of
Keith's friends that he introduced me to. You led me to
Prell Hall. I didn't want to go, if you remember, in fact
I'd refused to go with Keith a couple of times, then you
said it would be all right and promised to look after me.
Well . . ."

"Well?"

"Then," I said, "and there, up in the hills, in that terrible house, I discovered the _real_ Keith."

"Don't be melodramatic. It couldn't have been a complete surprise. Your adventure in Tijuana must have given
you a hint."

"I admit it should have, but—and I suppose this is
something disgustingly English coming out—I told myself it was in a foreign country and didn't really count." A
leaf from my crimson bougainvillea, riding on a spurt of
wind, settled mysteriously between front paws. "Anyway,
I want to know why you named it George."

"After my father."

"Really? You hardly ever mention him."

"He divorced my mother when I was seven and got custody of me because _she_ went off with another man— oddly enough, also named George. They're in South America now, running a coffee plantation."

"But what about George? Your father, not your step-father?"

Octavia shrugged.

"Is he strange and uninvited? Difficult to dispose of?"

"He's one of the thirty or however many it is men in America who made a million dollars by the time he was thirty-five. But we have nothing in common." Octavia sounded completely matter-of-fact, always a sign that hate was in the wings. "He makes a point of telephoning me on my birthday, and the call always comes through from some place like Madrid or Stockholm. It's to keep up the successful businessman image, I'm sure. Anyway, every birthday I get this message, this _warning_, to expect this long-distance call. I have to sit around waiting for it. Finally, over a lousy connection, I talk to this man who has nothing to say to me."

While she spoke, Octavia glared at the dog. The sun felt very warm. "The oddest thing of all," I said, "is you and I, sitting here on this beautiful morning, holding hands, looking at it, giving it names, and not doing anything at all about it."

"We're waiting for the police."

"_They_'ll find it odd if they arrive and see us here like this."

"I don't care. Keeping up appearances, especially in front of cops, doesn't interest me."

"You're right, Octavia."

"You bet you. This has become a very important day. I'm not usually introspective and I like to keep moving, but right now I'm taking stock. I'm giving myself the once-over. That's why I understand how *you* feel, my poor angel."

"Can I ask you something?"

"Shoot the works. I'm in the mood."

"What was it *like* in that shower?"

Octavia stood up, became the huntress again, poised on the threshold of an imaginary bathroom. "There was a great deal of steam. They'd closed the window and run the hot water for a while, so I saw them through a warm, damp mist. I'll spare you the obvious details, but it was a routine kind of a threesome—once I'd displaced Andy—after which we made coffee and had a discussion about it."

"A *discussion*? Hadn't you said it all?"

"You know the Prells. They're the kind who say, after they've done it, 'Man, we got a little bit nearer the truth that time.'"

"Pretentious gangbangs is all they are."

"In a way, I agree. But it all links up with a good deal that's going on in this country."

"Really? What's going on?"

She brushed away a fly as it passed her nose on its way to join others buzzing around dog. "Wife-swapping, for starters."

"But that's so middle class. They do it out in the suburbs, after a game of bridge."

"You're a snob, that's your problem. If you weren't, you'd see the whole syndrome for what it is." Impressive pause. "The old idea of one-to-one is breaking down,

45

Dora. However you _get there_, as they say, it's not through to have and to hold, for better or worse."

"I believe you have a point. Keith could never accept _me_ as the way of _getting there_."

"And you couldn't accept being just one way and not the _only_ way. We've been through this before, but if you and I ever had a serious relationship——"

"We won't, I don't want to, please don't talk about it."

"I'm kind of encouraged you fight it so hard. In the meantime, just take a look at homosexuals in general. They've been avant-garde for years. So many of them live together and have other people on the side, one of them goes away for a couple of months and it's taken for granted the other isn't going to just hang around being a grass widow. Stupid people call that promiscuous and take it as one more proof of how disgusting and unreliable they are. Nowadays, so-called normal life is following their example. And here's another point," Octavia said, her voice ringing across the canyon. "Why are so many people taking trips? It's because trips are getting to be a more popular way of _getting there_ than falling in love. Kids know all about this. Instead of having crushes, they hold marihuana parties. Rosemary's brother's in high school, he told her dozens of them not only take but make LSD after a few lessons in chemistry class. Last week his best friend was carried out on a stretcher, having hallucinations when he should have been listening to his math teacher."

"I agree this is new and interesting—much _more_ interesting than those dreary goings-on at Prell Hall, if you ask me——"

"I don't ask you, girl, and you're wrong. Will you never learn? Keith's one of *them*. But you've never accepted it. You never realized that if you wrote your autobiography it should be called, *I Married a Trip-Taker*."

"All right, Octavia. But why did he marry me?"

"He wanted a traveling companion."

"And I turned out to be an old stick-at-home?"

"You said it, I didn't."

"Oh God. Everything's too depressing."

Octavia glanced up the street. "And here come the cops. So pull yourself together, remember you're completely innocent this time, and stick to the point! Some stupid brute ran over some wretched dog and left it outside your door, so will they get off their asses and take it away?"

Officer Bates turned out to be disappointingly ordinary and polite. No cop-image, a lack of sun-goggles, tightly breeched thighs, sadistic mouth; but pale, fortyish and a little paunchy, with something apologetic, I felt, in the way he carried his holster. No doubt they assigned him only to mild cases, such as lost brooches, sprinklers that flood a neighbor's backyard, and dog trouble. He began by examining the body, pronouncing it dead, and asking me if I knew what it was. Octavia gave him a contemptuous look and retired to the living room. "It's almost a schipperke," I said. "Your true schipperke has no tail, so we must assume, in this case . . ." Officer Bates smiled faintly, muttered something about trouble in the barnyard, asked me how to spell schipperke, thanked me, and told me to think very hard before assuring him that I'd never seen the animal in question before. Still on the steps, I promised him that the dog was a stranger and listed the various hounds I knew in Bellavista Lane. He wrote all this down, glanced around, wanted to know how long the front gate had been broken. About a week, I said; and how? he asked; and remembering Octavia's advice to stick to the point, decided not to mention Keith and pretended I had no idea. This was a mistake. I couldn't tell whether Bates thought I was lying, but his eyes narrowed and he found it "unusual" that the gate hadn't been repaired. As I looked at him, the homely unassuming face became faceless; mask of officialdom was clamped over it, and I recognized the truth of earlier fears. In spite of cruelly deceiving first impressions, the person confronting me was an evil puppet stretched tight on the strings of dreadful official power.

"Shall we go into the house, officer? Since you've changed the subject, I see no point in standing on top of it out here."

He followed. Octavia, sitting in an armchair with Radclyffe at her feet, gave him another annihilating stare. I remained standing, no doubt defensively, for Bates had the nerve to tell me I was welcome to sit down. I chose the arm of Octavia's chair. He asked me why I'd waited so long to report the incident, Octavia gave me a warning tweak on the buttocks, and I tried to convey, as I answered, that he'd made it impossible to follow her advice. "Since you've already asked me about the front gate, and seem so interested in my personal life, I'll tell you." Managed a cool, offhand smile. "I happen to be in a slightly disturbed state of mind."

Noting this down, Bates denied any interest in my personal life but asked me to define what I meant. Did I suffer from mental blackouts? Was I under any kind of treatment? Had I ever been in an institution?

"No. But my husband left me, four days ago."

It became, I could tell, Bate's moment of triumph. The detective smiled. "Excuse me, Mrs. Poley, but did Mr. Poley break the front gate?"

"If you must know, he did. But not on purpose."

"An accident?"

"He happened to be annoyed about something, walked out of the house, slammed the gate and broke it. The gate is very old. The hinges are loose and the wood is partly warped."

"Why didn't you tell me this, Mrs. Poley, in the first place?"

"Because," said Octavia in her most commanding voice, "it's none of your damn business, Bates. We brought you here to deal with that thing outside. You've no right to snoop around the private life of an innocent woman."

I gave her an imploring pinch on the thigh. She caught my hand and held on to it. Bates told her not to interrupt; not to call him Bates; then, with an appalling suppressed smirk, found it "unusual" that I was practically sitting in Octavia's lap. I could only draw away guiltily, as they say, realizing that the man was beginning to believe he had a case. He'd marked us down as a pair of conniving dikes, Keith had left me on account of Octavia, and somehow we were using the dog to frame him. Nothing was too fantastic these days.

"Officer. I would like to ask *you* a question. Can you

understand that feeling when everything suddenly seems too much?"

He wrote this down and said, "No."

"No?"

"I can understand you're upset because your husband left you, Mrs. Poley. That's a terrible thing for any woman. But I don't see what it's got to do with waiting four hours to report a serious accident."

"Let me try and explain." I heard Octavia's exasperated sigh and turned my back on her. "I've been in this state in which any definite line of action has become . . . difficult. I'm still in it, by the way. Even quite simple things like going to the market or choosing what to wear become painful challenges. To put it bluntly, all my wheels are spoked. *Now*, can you imagine, feeling this way, waking up alone, finding what I found, out of nowhere, on my own front steps?"

A stare, and an offensively conciliating nod. "It kind of threw you, Mrs. Poley? I can understand that."

"Thank you. I sat and brooded and called a few friends on the phone before even trying to do anything about it. *I've* still done nothing about it, by the way. I owe everything to *them*. Miss Fell here called the Humane Society, who told her to call the police."

The eyes narrowed again. "Then why didn't she?"

"I beg your pardon?"

"Why didn't Miss Fell call the police? My record shows that a Mr. Chad Weston called, at 11:53 A.M."

Here it is, I thought; *it's coming; tightening of the mouth precedes official accusation; why not admit, Mrs. Poley, that in your disturbed state you ran over this in-*

nocent dog, then called up a couple of friends to help you out? Don't be afraid! The offense in itself is not serious. Accidents happen. Making a false statement to the police, however——

"Both Miss Fell and Mr. Weston," I said, "were kind enough to come over. _They_ understood my situation. After Miss Fell called the Humane Society, it was Mr. Weston's turn, so he called the police."

"I see." Professionally deadpan now, Bates noted all this down. I found his blankness worse than stealthy grin or wary eye. He cleared his throat. "Mrs. Poley, I can tell by your accent that you're British."

"Most people can."

"Are you here on a visit?"

"I live in your country."

"I see. I was in yours, once." Change of tactic didn't deceive me. A sudden, casual friendliness, I knew, was one of their favorite devices. Feeling more at home, you betrayed yourself. "During the war," Bates went on. "In Portsmouth. For a day."

"How did you find it?"

"I liked it."

"I'm very glad."

"Why did you leave England, Mrs. Poley?"

"One simply couldn't continue living there." (Had decided, now, to play his game.) "Things have perked up on the surface, of course—better food in restaurants, Mod clothes, Beatles, and so on—but I found an underlying sadness to it all. Nothing has _really_ changed, you see. We sink deeper into the past while flying a few gallant flags of the future."

_51_

"That's very interesting, Mrs. Poley. Thank you." He sounded almost respectful. "I like to hear about these things. I read an article recently that said England was sinking with a giggle into the ocean."

"I read it too, officer. And if one's destined to sink into the ocean, isn't it better to giggle?"

"That's very interesting. *How* did you leave England, Mrs. Poley?"

"I swam the Atlantic, officer. I was so desperate to get out." No smile; and I didn't really blame him. "Sorry. I flew to New York, stayed there a week, then rented a car and drove out here."

"I wasn't referring to methods of transportation, Mrs. Poley."

"Oh. You want a financial check-up? My grandfather, on my mother's side, who hadn't spoken to us for years because he disapproved of my mother marrying my father, died in 1964 and left me enough money to skip the country."

"So you're a resident alien?"

"That's right. With a green card."

"May I see it, please?"

"Stop torturing this woman," Octavia said as I left the room. "Stop bugging her about British accents and green cards when all she wants is to get that dog out of here." I didn't hear Bates's reply, but when I came back, she stood with her haughty back to him, smoking a cigarette and gazing out of the window. Bates observed that my card *seemed* to be in order, then reminded me almost jovially not to forget, being a foreigner, that I must report next month to the Post Office and fill out my annual form. I promised. Octavia drew in breath with an impatient hiss. "For Christ's sake get on with it, Bates. It's Christmas tomorrow."

"I was coming to that," said Bates. She turned around to stare at him. "You won't get anyone to come around on a national holiday, and the Humane Society closes early today." Thought I detected grimace of satisfaction as he glanced at watch. "We've got three hours to trace that dog's owner, or we'll have to hold over until after the celebrations."

"It's not possible!" I said.

Bates looked surprised. "Don't give up, Mrs. Poley. We can do a lot in three hours."

"I didn't mean that. I meant, if you fail, no one will take that dog away for another forty-eight."

"Oh, you can move it, Mrs. Poley. You mustn't destroy it, because it's evidence, but you can move it."

Octavia walked slowly toward him. "There's no room in the refrigerator, Bates. If you fail, we'll have to take steps. I don't care if you press charges. In fact, I'd welcome a test case, just to show you all up."

"We'll do what we can," said Bates, "as quickly as we can." To Octavia: "Take it easy, miss." To me: "Nice talking to you, Mrs. Poley." Mask of officialdom clamped down even more firmly, he left.

Octavia smokes a special kind of cigarette that comes from New York in boxes. Between the two layers of cigarettes, there's an order blank; she removed this now, disclosing two or three joints carefully spaced out on the lower level. She lit up and we passed the joint back and forth in silence, four or five times, winking or grinning occasionally at each other. At the first drag I was still fairly panic-stricken, visions of trial and deportation swirling around my head; at the last—delicious last, tapering joint held between the blades of my nail scissors so that not a puff should be wasted—I began to feel the interview had gone better than could possibly have been expected. "God, Octavia! I admired your hostility to that man, I'm sure you scared the shit out of him, but there *is* another way of dealing with them, you know. I mean, introducing the human element. Our little talk about why I left England genuinely interested him. I believe in a certain sense it turned the tide. Up to that moment, in his eyes, I was some kind of freak or hysteric, lying through my teeth, building my own cage and then clawing at the bars like a terrified rabbit. Then he discovered a very simple, moving fact. I actually preferred America—*his* country—to my own, because it had given me something England never could give me."

"Keith?"

"Sometimes you *are* a bitch but I don't mind. I can get through this thing. I'm convinced of that now. Even if I've lost Keith forever, and I'm not sure I have, I'll survive."

"Good girl. Let's do one more."

When she gets stoned, Octavia doesn't talk much. I tend to soliloquize, but she retires (like Keith) to a contented private place. She glanced out of the window now, murmured "Landscape with Dog" in a calmly cheerful way, walked over to the phonograph and played an album by the Tijuana Brass. Naturally I was back at the border, at the end of our first day, beginning of our second evening. Keith had asked me to drive back; the moment they let us into California, after a very perfunctory search of the car, I realized why. He took the little sack of marihuana from one pocket, a pack of Bambū papers from another, and rolled a joint. "It's not waiting room or church or flophouse," he said, "so try it now."

"Won't it affect my performance at the wheel?"

Mainly because I was resisting it, the drug had no effect whatsoever. Also, another storm arrived from the Pacific. I had to concentrate on dark, crowded highway beyond streaming windshield while Keith switched on the radio, leaned back in his seat and stared at the roof, seemingly unaware of night, rain, halts at stop lights, certainly unaware of me. I thought of an island, surrounded by empty ocean and far, flat horizon. He had the relaxation that comes only from deliberate aloneness, for being with another person demanded attitudes and tensions, that wearisome business of feeling something. When I refused a third drag, he seemed almost relieved; it was as if I consigned myself to the horizon, a comfortably distant speck from Crusoe's point of view.

A silence lasted for perhaps an hour. This time I felt no desire to break it and had the dignified sulks instead, with no effect on Keith at all. A flash of lightning, and I regretted my performance at the bullfight but refused to hold anything else against myself; a mild thunderclap, and I brooded over Keith's enjoyment of that seedy brothel in the mountains and his indifference to a screaming kitten; then drew comfort from the thought that polarities attract.

He turned the radio down. "I'd like you to meet the Prells."

Being spoken to after such a long, unsatisfactory intermission was confusing. "Who are they?"

"Brothers. We had this conversation before."

"Oh yes. I unwittingly described their house."

"Superficially."

"Why should I meet them?"

"To get below the surface."

"And what's it like down there?"

"No demands are made."

"I know that appeals to _you_. I never said it did to _me_."

"You honestly enjoy being bothered?"

"I don't think I think in those terms. I think of people needing each other, a kind of fair exchange."

"People not needing each other is fair exchange, too."

Another silence lasted maybe forty-five minutes. Then he asked if I wanted a cigarette.

"Which kind?"

He grinned. "Regular."

"Thank you."

He lit one for me and put it between my lips. "Have you been involved with anyone recently?"

"A week after I arrived in California, last year, I began a love affair."

"Who was he?"

"An actor."

"Go on."

"Not famous. Struggling. We were together ten months, but I never saw him work so I've no idea if he was talented."

"I'll bet he was."

"Why?"

"You wouldn't be attracted to someone who wasn't."

"That's the first compliment you've paid me. Of course, you're complimenting yourself at the same time."

"Tell me what went wrong."

"All the clichés about actors are true. They're impossible to resist until you discover their selfishness is beyond belief. On the other hand, when they hit a run of bad luck you see how vulnerable and helpless they are. They resent this terribly, and with good reason, but if you can't help them, they resent you, too."

"Were you hurt?"

"A bit."

"There's always one who gets hurt and one who hurts."

"Always?"

No answer to this, but another question. "What are you like when you're hurt?"

"Miserable, of course."

"But do you suffer in silence? Are you good at sudden reproachful looks and long, desperate walks?"

"No, Keith. I speak out."

"Then why didn't you?"

"When?"

Put his arm along the back of my seat, rested his hand lightly on my shoulder. "You've been furious with me ever since we left Mexico. Why didn't you say something?"

"Oh God, I don't know where I am with you."

A song came over the radio, and immediately deflected him. "Listen to this. It's great."

57

Found a shell on the beach
Broke like a promise
Saw a bird in the sky
Flew off like hope
Heard a sound in the air
Disappear

"Beautiful," Keith said.

"Yes, it's one of my favorites, too."

"Tell me the others."

" 'Elusive Butterfly.' 'Who am I?' 'Call me.' 'Nowhere Man.' "

"Beautiful."

"What?"

"Those titles. Like bottles washed up on a beach, each with a different message inside."

At one in the morning, we reached his house. My car stood outside, silhouette of neighbor's boat looming beyond it. Storm had cleared and the moon was out, ringed with bright clouds. Having slept for the last hour, Keith awoke as I switched off the engine. He seemed momentarily astonished at my presence; said, "Okay"; took his key-ring from the ignition; kissed me on the cheek and opened his door. "Good night, Dora."

Unbelieving, I sat with my hands on the steering wheel until he reached the front door. Then I honked the horn twice.

Moon full on his face, he turned around. He looked very young, sleepy, mystified. "Something wrong?"

"Of course not. I just wanted to say good night."

He stared at me for a moment. "Speak out, Dora."

"But I have nothing to say, now that I realize that somewhere along the line I've been deeply misled. I had the impression that possibly we meant something to each other. I see it was mistaken, and am struck dumb."

A smile. "Dumb Dora?" When I didn't answer, he came back to the car and leaned through the open window. "You want to go through the I-care-about-you-of-course-we're-going-to-see-a-lot-of-each-other kind of shit?"

"I suppose I expected a bit of that kind of shit."

"I'm sorry."

"So am I."

"You think I don't adore you?" Sudden, disconcertingly flirtatious smile. "I truly adore you." Held my hand. "But don't expect me to do anything about it."

"What does that mean?"

"If it's going to happen, it's going to happen."

"I see." Saw only the expression on his face, convinced that he'd made his point and I must be crazy not to acknowledge it.

"Okay. You want to stay over?"

"Do you want me to?"

"Jesus!" Let go my hand. "You _don't_ see."

"I'm sorry."

He started to open the door for me. "Please don't bother," I said calmly, "I prefer to do that for myself." A shrug, and he walked back to the house. I loitered deliberately on the sidewalk, gazing at the wasteland under the moon. Oil pump shuttled; someone zoomed by on a motor-bike, mildly neanderthal in crash-helmet. I entered my own car and sat in it for perhaps a minute, listening

to the thud of surf, getting a headache. Saw that the front
door had been left open and got out again; found Keith
on the bed, asleep in his clothes; searched for pencil
and paper and found that, too; wrote "CALL ME," stuck
the note in an empty wine bottle and drove indignantly
home.

Telephone rang. Octavia ignored it.

"Mrs. Poley?" Voice sounded like a child's.

"No."

"Well, tell her I got a clue but I can't follow it up yet."

"Who is this?"

"Greg."

"The one with a bicycle, working for a dollar?"

"That's right. Who is this?"

"Mrs. Poley."

"Why d'you say it wasn't? Expecting someone nasty
to call?"

"Always."

"Well, I'm in a phone booth. Down in the canyon, at
the service station. A guy who works here told me he's
often seen a funny black dog wandering around by itself."

"Does he know who it belongs to?"

"That's the trouble. Some old couple on Palermo Drive,
and nobody answers. Nobody barks, though, and I guess
that's encouraging."

"Yes. Thank you so much, Greg."

"You're welcome. We'll get to the bottom of this."

"I hope so."

"And I can always use an extra dollar."

He hung up. I looked at Octavia. She smiled, less at me than at some pleasantly hallucinated world of her own; and I decided to go out. Half a joint had been definitely bracing, I felt confident now that my test would work, would take a drive and find dog gone when I returned. After all, things were moving. Greg and Bates between them would clear the matter up, Keith had promised to come to the party, no need to wake in tears on Christmas morn. Octavia approved my decision, and asked if she might stay where she was. Enjoying it here, she said, had nothing special to do, didn't feel like hitting the road yet, might turn on some more and think about Rosemary, life, etc. We kissed. I ran down steps, said inner farewell to dog, took down top of Ghia and drove out into world.

Spinning up the coast highway in dark glasses, I enjoyed sparkle of ocean, winter sun-worshippers on the pale beaches, gaudy little hot-dog stands under looming cliffs. A solitary white sailboat, moving very slowly, was the most appealing of all. It became first an image of loneliness, so pure, exquisite and distant; then an invitation to a voyage. I stepped on the gas and wondered where to go. After all, I could get on a plane tonight. Not Mexico—too booked-up; not Hawaii—ditto, and common at Christmastime; Hong Kong might be original, Bangkok even more so. In a sense, destination didn't matter. What mattered was standing Keith up, the whole pack of them saying as they piled into their cars, "Oh God, we've got to go to Dora's party, she'll kill herself if we don't," arriving in front of an empty house with possibly a rude note pinned to the gate.

At Malibu pier I turned around and began speeding back. Still no destination in mind, only not going home. Saw the sailboat again. It looked forlorn this time, pointless and lost. Felt certain I could do better, and at some point entered a freeway, enjoyed losing myself in its shifting abstractions, nipping in and out of lanes for the sheer aesthetic pleasure of changing traffic-composition. _Absolutely under control,_ by the way. (Would even advise people taking driving tests to smoke a little of the stuff first, it firms up expertise and confidence, cuts down the Examiner to size.) After a while, the landscape changed; became personal instead of abstract; I recognized the narrow winding road that climbed the hill to Prell Hall, and had to admit my intentions to myself. Even so, they weren't clear.

The house was Hollywood Gothic, built in the twenties, a large gray concoction of archways, turrets, buttresses, balconies, and attic windows like motionless, watchful eyes. Driveway skirted a fountain, as usual not playing. Somebody's shorts were drying on the rim of the bowl. Three cars were parked outside, Keith's Triumph, Jim's old refurbished Cadillac, Andy's racing-green souped-up Dodge. Obviously a white elephant, the place had been bought simply as headquarters for official way-outness. The brothers, twenty-six and twenty-seven, tall and handsome in a clean-cut way, like men's fashion models in superior magazines who happen _not_ to be wearing the expected non-wrinkle acrylic raincoat or two-button natural-contour blazer, were sons of a shrewd, retired movie star. She'd done well in real estate and a chain of markets that sold organically grown food. Officially, Jim and Andy were partners in both these enterprises, pricing a house or a lot from time to time, I suppose, or making an occasional trip up the coast to inspect apple orchards; basically, they were friends, hosts and procurers (introductions free, psychedelics C.O.D.) to the protest-song crowd. Musicians, staying at the house while they gave a concert in Los Angeles, often left small traces or mementos there —guitar, roll of tape, dark glasses, stranded member of an entourage. The shorts on the fountain, probably, were in this category. For some reason, they interested me. After parking, I walked over to inspect them, found POLEY on the laundry tag, and reflected that Keith himself might now be in this category, too. I left them where I found them.

Front door was off the latch, so I walked straight in. The house seemed completely silent, my footsteps echoed across the bare hallway leading to a vast, dim living room. Whiff of sandalwood greeted me, still sweetening the air after last night's fumes, floating like an echo. (They always lit incense to overlay the stink of hemp.) Venetian blinds shut out most of the afternoon; pieces of furniture lay around like islands on a sea of polished wood—leather armchair, Early American wing chair, ancient couch, love seat, archipelago of colored throw-pillows near the fireplace. On the coffee table, an empty half-gallon of red wine, and beside it a half-full glass which, settling on the love seat, I polished off. Lit cigarette and watched smoke circle toward the high, beamed ceiling. As I remembered my only visit here—Keith my escort, Octavia my duenna—figures materialized like ghosts on throw-pillows and couch, "Queen Jane Approximately" drifted from a phonograph, afternoon turned without effort (because of the closed blinds) to night.

Nobody looked up or acknowledged us as we arrived. Nothing unfriendly about this, just an assumption that we belonged and would find our rightful places, would join other contented shadows. Keith, angry because I'd said I wouldn't go with him, then changed my mind at Octavia's insistence, abandoned me at once. I saw him sit beside a dark-haired girl on the floor. She wore a sweatshirt with BRAHMS printed across it, great composer's face staring from her breasts. She smiled and offered Keith a drag of her cigarette. Octavia held my hand, pointed out a famous young singer, wild-haired and thin, admired and surrounded, telling a story with long, gesturing hands and an occasional rasping, bitter laugh. A girl with heavy earrings and a black cape drifted by, winked at Octavia, sank into the leather armchair and closed her eyes. From nowhere, as it seemed, a gleaming silver shape floated in the air toward her, hesitated, and rested on the arm of her chair. Octavia explained that it was a pillow filled with helium. The girl seemed unaware of it. It waited, absolutely still. Then somebody walked past. It followed him. He joined a group on a windowseat. It sank to the floor, and waited again.

Jim Prell appeared, barefoot, wearing faded levis and an unbuttoned denim shirt: something disconcertingly eager and innocent in his friendly eyes, perfect teeth and lithe body. After Octavia's introduction, he decided to take me in hand, poured me a glass of slightly sweet red wine and suggested we sit on the floor. Octavia joined Keith and the dark-haired girl. I looked at Jim. He smiled, and seemed, like the pillow, to be waiting. I commented politely on the house. He agreed it was great. We began smoking. The singer's laugh grated across the room. "Blowin' in the Wind" came from the phonograph. A chandelier with only one light burning glimmered above our heads.

Determined not to appear an outsider, I took a series of expert, quick, panting drags, like a thirsty dog. They registered well, for Jim asked at once if I'd tried peyote. Not yet, I said, and wondered how it compared with mescaline; the greatest, he said with his winning, almost college-boy smile, really the greatest. But had I not taken mescaline? (Expression of genuine, direct astonishment here.) Oh yes, I lied. And did I have a good time? Oh, I freaked out. What did I discover? What one discovered, I informed him—improvising and rather enjoying it now —was much less important than what one felt; prefer possibilities to certainties, have found that the inner vision catches fire while the external act merely freezes. Like the hashish we're smoking now, Jim said. Having thought it was only ordinary, less drastic marihuana, I endured a moment of panic, then nodded agreement and smoked some more. The phonograph sang, "Don't Think Twice." Hours were becoming an exciting blur, with occasional contrasts of extreme clarity: twice, silence took over the whole room like a palpable force and it seemed huge, suspended, like a moving film stop-framed; the separation between notes on someone's guitar sounded unbearably sharp and cutting; the quiet, single light on the chandelier seemed to contain mysterious power and could never be put out; and the helium pillow suddenly glimmered at our feet. Jim jumped up, the pillow rose with him, he went into a bullfight-act with it, making passes and stabs. I cried *"Olé!"* and when he sat down again, said, "You cunning little bastard," and embraced him. I saw two boys necking, which led to my speech about the Heterosexual and Society, which went down very well (with the few who listened), and again established me as more cool than expected. "Dora, here's another roach," Jim said, and I burned my mouth on the butt.

"Blowin' in the Wind" again and Jim with his arm around me as Keith walked past, his face beautifully content. I looked up at him and he rested his hand on my shoulder in a gesture of such tender, complete reconciliation that I kissed his fingers, told them I loved him. I noticed his eyes had lost their usual fierceness. He said something that I didn't understand, about a connection between his own name and the music on the phonograph. Jim, both arms around me now, explained that Keith in Gaelic meant "the wind." I laughed; looked up at Keith again, still holding on to his hand, enjoying the softness of his eyes; I said, "So it bloweth where it listeth, I presume," and he nodded, withdrew his fingers gently, brushed my cheek with the back of his hand and moved away. The dark-haired girl joined him and they disappeared.

Before I had time to think about it, Octavia came and knelt at my feet. She asked Jim if I wasn't marvelous, and Jim agreed, and so did I. They joked about the surprise of Keith marrying anyone, but felt I was the inevitable choice—the English seem so grand and unwilling, but can really give Americans a lesson or two, and wasn't

I Keith's lesson or two? They explored and stroked me a good deal. I encouraged this, not really responding to an individual (or two) but to moves in a game of initiation. The feeling continued as we found ourselves in a large dark bedroom which contained only a large dark bed, which contained the three of us, naked. "It's really not bad here at all," I remarked, and laughed, and made (and meant) sounds of pleasure. Then I saw the chandelier with one light burning glide across the room. I pushed Octavia and Jim away, got out of bed, ran naked to the door, crying: "If we're really together, why are we apart?" and _had_ to find Keith at once.

Wandering down passageways that seemed monstrously long, opening doors, closing them again, hearing cruel sounds of a guitar from downstairs, I eventually saw him in a similar room, in a similar bed, with the dark-haired girl. Little burglar-light fixture glowed from the wall, caught BRAHMS on her sweatshirt discarded on the floor. The anguish was unspeakable. "The act may be absurd," I shouted, "but the intention is insulting!" and was appalled when they took no notice. After more passageways, encountered a small, narrow staircase obviously leading nowhere; climbed it; and entered a huge unlighted bathroom with (surprisingly enough) a bidet, on which I crouched; became sullen and somber; was haunted by an image of my mother dead on that beach, remembered Keith asking me once why she killed herself, and my reply: "I don't know. I don't know _if_ she did. I suppose she did. I never really asked anyone. From something my father said years later, I gathered the marriage had been a sexual disaster. She was marvelous, he said, but a puritan." Keith gave his sudden, clever, observer's smile. "Is that where you get it from?" Now, in this bathroom, at the top of this horrible mansion, I understood the whole conspiracy. The evening was an assault on what they all considered my puritanism, a collusion of Keith, Octavia and Prells. Heard people calling my name but ignored them, sitting and trembling in darkness until I threw up, felt better, and had fierce longings for food. Octavia, finding me in a kitchen, scrambling eggs, stark naked, asked if I was all right.

She claims that's when it happened, alleges that I implored her to go away and let me eat in peace, but she stayed, allowed me my eggs, bided her time, and I threw myself in her arms. *I* remember that she left; I ate, wept, wandered, went to sleep somewhere; was awakened by her voice, breath and hands, felt too overwhelmed to resist. Anyway, I didn't enjoy it.

Someone approached. Footsteps echoed like mine across the hallway. I stood up, and tried to retreat into shadows; it was too late, and during a moment of ridiculous irritation I felt clumsy, guilty, unfairly surprised. *Muffed my entrance; should have been discovered in position of strong, enigmatic calm, not caught like a prowler.* I pretended to pour wine, shook a last reluctant drop from the flagon and sat down again.

Keith wore a black alpaca sweater I'd given him, and black shorts; looked tired, or maybe hungover from the previous night. I'd expected a frown, or at least some gesture of disapproval when he saw me, but received instead a vague and lenient smile.

"Hello."

"Hello. Keith, I honestly don't know why I came."

Gave me a sidelong glance. "Is it so important to have a reason?"

"Well, I suppose—as a general rule—one likes to be able to explain one's actions."

He laughed. "My life's made up of unexplained actions. If I started analyzing them one by one, my hair would turn gray before I finished."

"From the effort or the time involved?"

"We're sharp today."

"I'm sorry. I didn't mean to be." _Going wrong already?_ "I went out for a drive, you see, started up the coast, turned back and . . . found myself here. Of course I came to see _you_, I can't honestly say I didn't. But I've no idea why."

Another glance, thinking it over. "May I venture a simple explanation?"

"Please. It would be such a relief."

"You wanted to see me."

"Yes, but . . ." I trailed off, feeling I'd muffed my opening scene as well as my entrance. Also, there was something disconcerting about Keith today; he was being more reasonable than I. The experience was so novel that I found it, obscurely, a threat.

"Anyway, I'm glad you wanted to see me."

"Truly?"

"Sure." The smile again, not cunning but friendly and tolerant. Maybe it was just fatigue and too much pot. "We don't have to go through all that I-hate-you-I-never-want-to-see-you-again shit. Do we?"

"I hope not."

"Like a drink?"

"Thank you. Red wine, if it's handy."

He grinned. "Around here, it's got to be." Disappeared, leaving me a minute to wonder what I was hoping for. Reconciliation? Not yet, if ever. Assurance that I wasn't utterly loathsome to him? Perhaps. (And it seemed that I wasn't.) Clue as to how he felt after four days without me? Impossible—four days mean nothing after ten months of marriage, and he'd be on his guard, anyway. Next problem: what was *he* hoping for, now that I'd come to see him? Apparently wanted me to stay, otherwise why offer me a drink? Then——

A door creaked, and Keith returned with a bottle of wine and a can of beer, handed me the bottle, sprawled opposite me in the leather chair, examined something unsatisfactory on his left leg.

"Keith, you look tired. Heavy night?"

His eyelids flickered. "No. No one special here, just Octavia, Rosemary, Mark, Andy and Jim. Spent most of the time bullshitting with Jim."

"I had the impression, when I called this morning, that the usual crowd——"

"No." A touch of impatience. "How typical you should assume that."

It was true I'd heard only one voice, or sound, that didn't belong to Keith or Octavia. "I suppose it is. I admit it."

"Are we meek and mild today?"

"No." I smiled. "And we're not sharp, either. To be honest, I don't know what we are."

"That's the third time you said 'honestly' or 'to be honest.'"

"Really?"

The same smile. "Makes me suspicious."

"I call that typical, too."

"Okay."

A silence. He drank beer from the can. I poured more wine. "Keith, I'd like to bring up something, if I may."

Waved a lordly hand. "You may."

"Octavia mentioned that you were discussing me last night—does that come under the heading of bullshitting, or not, I wonder? Anyway, she told me you brought up my silly lie about the bullfight, and said there were a dozen other instances."

He looked genuinely distressed. "Dora, it's not important."

"Maybe not to you. It matters to me."

"Don't let it. I only brought it up because I was in a mood to hold something against you."

"Oh."

"And I know all your lies came out of a kind of concern for what I'd think of you."

"Excuse me. _All_ my lies?" Knew I was risking a pointless quarrel, but the touch of patronage infuriated me. "That's a sweeping statement, Keith."

"I don't have a check-list handy, so I'll bring up one more and then let's drop it. You wanted to be so in and cool that night here, so you pretended to Jim you'd taken mescaline."

"Well, I admit that was stupid. But a group like that, when you're an outsider, is very intimidating. And _you_

71

must admit you didn't help me. You abandoned me the moment we came in the room, and . . ." I thought of his hand on my shoulder that night, and what it meant to me; his bewilderment when I found it so painful afterward, a kind of Judas-kiss. *"What do you mean, betrayal? I was just telling you that whatever I might do, or you might do, didn't matter."*

He was frowning at his left leg.

"What's the matter with it, Keith?"

"Funny kind of a little white spot. Come and look."

He twisted around, extending a deeply tanned calf. I knelt on the floor to examine it, and could find nothing. He took my hand, guided it to a minuscule patch. "Oh yes. It's a little fungus one picks up at the beach. Nothing serious."

We looked at each other, hands still linked.

"What should I do about it?" Keith asked.

"The Prells have a doctor, I imagine. Ask him for a prescription."

He let go my hand. I returned to the love seat and drank more wine. "I'm glad my lies aren't important," I said. "They're not why you left me?"

He shook his head. "That's what I told you. And in spite of what I said to Octavia last night, I don't hold *anything* against you. I admire and respect you very much." Gave me a direct, appraising, candid look. "You're attractive and intelligent and funny, but you just happen to be unlivable-with."

"Oh God." It was like a blow in the face. "Is that your last word?"

"There are no last words."

"Then I wish there were. A last word after *that* last word would wipe me out."

"It wasn't a criticism." Expression of deep surprise. "All I meant was, *I* can't live with you."

"Why?"

"Because I hurt you. When I hurt people, I've got to withdraw."

"It's as simple as that?"

"Yes. You can talk your way in and out of anything, and it sounds great, but you're a hopeless and scared little romantic who needs total attention, physical and otherwise. If you don't get it, you think you're losing your grip."

"Well! It may not be criticism, but it's devastating. Another word for all you've just said is, egotist."

"I didn't say it. But I guess I hurt you again, which proves my point. All I meant was, you're scared of the Prells, and this house, because there's a kind of freedom here and you can't accept it. You take it as a personal threat."

"My one experience here was highly unpleasant. But setting that aside, Keith—what *is* this freedom? What's so free about sitting around, turning on, sometimes getting into bed with each other—and never really committing yourself to anything? Just bullshitting, as you call it."

"It's an attitude. Do what you like and don't worry about who cares, who judges. Whatever happens, happens. Tomorrow it didn't happen, unless you really wanted it to." He smiled. "I like that. It suits me."

Upstairs, I heard a door slam. I got up. "I hope today didn't happen tomorrow."

"Okay. But don't look like that. I never want to offend you, Dora. How's the dog?"

"Still there when I left."

"Are they working on it?"

"Oh yes. And I hope I didn't make it sound too much of a Thing over the phone. It doesn't seem that way any more. Whatever happens, happens—that's how I feel about it now."

He opened the front door. "See you tomorrow then."

"You really want to come?" I stared at him. "Really?"

"I'll be there."

"You could still call it off, I suppose."

"Why?" Kissed me on the cheek. "Sounds like a good party."

As I moved away past the empty fountain, I glanced into the driving mirror; saw him standing outside the house. Turned into the street and the mirror-image tilted, rows of intent windows went askew, house loomed above his figure now seated on a bench, apparently staring at the sky. Instinct, that overrated faculty, had brought me to him, then abandoned me. Dumped me, so to speak, in my hour of need, and left me to drive home wondering if it could be true that I, Dora Poley, am unlivable-with? Admired and respected, but not loved? Had plenty of time to consider these gloomy questions, because the freeway was choked with traffic. Under a declining sun, one of a thousand beetles crawling along, I pitied, doubted and justified myself.

The house and home I made for Keith (draining the rest of my legacy), wasn't that a gesture of faith and love? For when he asked me to marry him, he warned me not to expect a house. The proposal was quite sudden, fairly reluctant, on Olvera Street, in the downtown Mexican quarter. I'd watched him photograph fashion models posed against bright quaint stalls; he finished work, took my arm, we sat at an outdoor café table and ordered Margueritas. "You've been blackmailing me for two months."

"What, Keith? That's not true. How?"

"We have a good time together, but you always leave me feeling I've disappointed you somehow." And, before I could protest: "So we've either got to stop seeing each other, or get married. Which do you prefer?"

In a case like this, I said, I'll choose the easy way out. If a simple formality enables us to go on seeing each other, why not accept it? He agreed, then added there'd be no house. Not that he couldn't afford one; but simply didn't wish to buy one, disliked making plans, was not the kind of person who needed to put down roots. I wondered, since he'd now actually made one plan, which was to marry me, and we'd both have to put down roots somewhere, would he object if _I_ bought a house and _he_ came to live in it? He shrugged. "I guess I'd be in no position to. But don't ask me to help you find it. I don't want any part of that." Duly encouraged, I settled on 167 Bellavista Lane, painted its walls and planted its earth. "I'll pay for our bed, my darkroom, and what I consider other essentials," Keith said. "Food and liquor, things to sit on and eat off. The rest, like property taxes and decorator's shit, is up to you."

On my hands, then, a creature partially wild (in the literal sense of being improperly domesticated); still in

75

revolt, I presumed, against his original home, that family and place I found endlessly mysterious because he talked so little about it. Of the Poley clan, he invited only Malowaka to our wedding. She caught the flu and couldn't make it. In a sense, because I often thought of her as a rival, I was relieved; in another, I was sorry, for she might have provided the last supremely incongruous touch. Keith and I tied our knot on the balcony of a hotel suite in Hollywood. It belonged to Octavia, who'd recently arrived from New York and hadn't found an apartment yet. She rented a clergyman and bought champagne. The guest list, at Keith's insistence, was minimal: Prells (groom) and Chad Weston (bride). I wore a white leotard, Keith slipped into brown hopsack levis and a thin red sweater. By contrast, Jim and Andy (jackets, open-necked shirts, shoes but no socks) looked almost formal. Chad, with a boutonniere in his suit, disapproved on all counts. He wished me happiness as if it were the last thing in the world I might expect, gulped a glass of champagne, explained he had to drive immediately to Santa Barbara to stay the weekend on someone's ranch, and said, "Well, D.P., you must bring him to dinner soon." Clergyman left with him and Prells at once handed round joints. We smoked blatantly, leaning over the balcony and watching guests in the hotel pool splashing about below.

Anxious for us not to miss the plane for Las Vegas, which Keith said was beautiful, a gambling city, the perfect place for honeymooners, I pretended to take more drags than I actually did. That night, after I'd won $7.50 on a one-arm bandit and Keith lost nearly $100 at keno, and we'd gone to bed, and I couldn't sleep at all, I thought of Malowaka's wedding gift. Appropriately enough, it was a gadget, one of those devices that wake you up in the morning and have a cup of hot coffee ready. To me, the grandmother was the most real of Keith's connections; I'd seen the picture of her in ceremonial feathers, knew of her house, tent and addiction to kitchen appliances, knew that she'd struck oil and Keith loved her. Octavia and Prells, though, I knew only slightly, and father and mother he'd kept, deliberately, a remote inauspicious blur. So, while he lay buried in delta, I imagined a squat brick house in Montrose, Colorado; two people standing un-hopefully outside it, as in paintings by Edward Hopper; a porch, a cottonwood tree, a relentless sky. On this wedge of land, containing five thousand or so inhabitants, mountain range to one side and scrub desert to the other, Mr. Poley Senior sold insurance policies and was perenni-ally unfaithful to his wife.

Later, rifling Keith's desk in my house one day, I found a photograph of them. They seemed what is usually called a handsome pair, husband sturdy and genial-looking, wife recognizable as Malowaka's daughter through flattish face and cavernous eyes. When the picture was taken, they couldn't have been married long. Mrs. Poley Senior had yet to begin weeping at dinner; running off with her little son to Malowaka on the reservation, where more Scotch than sympathy was dispensed; taking him along, too, when she surprised the adulterer with his secretary in a rented room; cursing or pleading or trying to invade the once conjugal bed; sending a rival something unmention-able through the mail. This hell, I gathered from Keith, still endured. He thanked God he hadn't been there in years, but Malowaka, who obviously despised her daughter and was entertained by her humiliations, kept him up to date.

Knowing, then, from the start exactly which foot I could put wrong, I walked (I thought) with care. Accepted overnight visits to Prell Hall and other more temporary habits, such as photographing nude females in our bedroom and asking me to watch and comment (this, allegedly, for a book that was later abandoned). I welcomed all comers and cooked excellent meals for them, retiring cheerfully to bed when they turned on and bullshitted through the small hours; avoided questions and scenes, except for the night I was Micky-Finned that hashish cigarette; was friendly both to long silences and endless grandmother anecdotes; openly pledged support, and donation, to a local campaign to legalize marihuana. Still, in the end, I met only rejection and failure.

Four nights ago, an hour before dawn, Keith arrived home. Unfortunately I was awake, for pills had recently begun to fail me. When I said nothing, he accused me of suffering in silence. Made no comment on this. Could I *deny* that he made me suffer? A little, sometimes, I admitted; but could *he* deny that I made as little of it as possible? This wasn't, according to him, the point. If I suffered at all, it meant that in spite of marriage he continued to disappoint me. "Keith, I don't know why you want to argue, but my only disappointment is that after almost a year you're still testing me. It causes a certain dreary tension between us. May I not be allowed to flunk or make the grade? If I'm to be your guinea pig forever, it's not marriage—it's vivisection."

Saw at once that I'd gone too far. (My clarity, I know, is occasionally mistaken for coldness.) He became speechless with anger and retired to the bathroom. After that, a toilet flushed, a door slammed and a gate broke.

Back from world, parked outside the drooping gate at sunset; noticed first that Octavia's car had gone, then that dog hadn't. Light was glassy clear as it faded, black body seemed to harden and congeal. Brushing against it by mistake, I found this not optical illusion but fact. Rigor mortis had set in, paws clenched and foxlike head stiff as a trophy on the wall.

In the living room, a note waited: *Remembered last minute Xmas shopping. Greg says old couple still not at home, no word from idiot cops. Love, O.* For lack of anything better to do, I turned on garden sprinklers, realizing that dog would be soaked, but couldn't see that it mattered. As the water hissed, I stood by the window and watched a blazing sunset over the Pacific. In winter, California colors become summery. No haze to dredge away brilliance and intensity, but green of trees, blue of ocean, bird-of-paradise orange and bougainvillea crimson stand out vividly tropical. Since there are few deciduous trees, anyway, you might even overlook the change of season. After sludge, freeze and bareness of English winters, personally welcome this. Also, it abstracts time. The basic flow is undisturbed. Arrival of coolness and sudden, concentrated periods of rain are not enough to interrupt it. The zone here is temperate, the climate's even keel makes people facile and optimistic; and the unexpected, by contrast, is doubly so. Hence, I believe, enormous shock of my dog problem, which enters the category not only of *shouldn't happen*, but *shouldn't happen here*. Believe, too, that my refusal to move the remains in spite of police permission, my continual outraged, cryptic stares, are protest against a violation of the rules.

Pause of dusk, warning of night, is in any case momentous. At this point, especially so; while I remain on my empty stage, like an actress who refuses to go home after the curtain's come down, my friends have left the theater. Chad searches for another beautiful, disastrous adventure, Octavia goes back to pursuing Rosemary and routing Andy. My husband, who admires and respects but will not live with me, sits in Prell Hall anticipating hours of supreme bullshit. This time I shall send out no signals. I shall wait. In the past, strength has been summoned and arrived like a prompt servant. I ring the bell for it now, alone on a canyon's rim with a dead body, a lost love, and a low, outrageous, lopsided moon.

Night; last glow of sun over the ocean has vanished; ocean has vanished, too; moon a feeble yellow. Lights spring up as if the whole canyon were a candelabrum with a hundred branches. Not a breath of wind. Out of stillness and darkness, any sound becomes inflated. Someone hammers half a mile away and it sounds like next door. And my own telephone rings louder than a burglar alarm.

Expecting Greg, or perhaps Octavia, I answer and hear the voice of my neighbor, Mrs. Cody, she who casts a cold eye on glamor stocks, believes in driving crime off the streets and into the prisons, wiping out pornography and junkies, spraying napalm on disobedient natives, and is a customer of the Fragile look. This afternoon, when I was out, she drove home and happened to notice dog. She examined it, found it dead, and demands an explanation. Whose is it, why is it there, have I no sense of decency? Wearily, I give her the facts. There are moments, she reminds me, when we must take the law into our own hands, and suggests this is one of them. I agree, but confess my inability to hatch up anything. Her voice grows alarmed, hostility mellows into concern. *Are you all right? Is something the matter with you? I wondered about you when I saw you sitting on the steps with that young woman. And I haven't seen Mr. Poley in days! Where is Mr. Poley?*

Checked out, I say. We're up the creek. Please don't worry. *But it's Christmas! Isn't that terrible for you?* Not really, I'm giving a party tomorrow. *Still, it won't be the same without Mr. Poley, will it?* Certainly it will. Mr. Poley's coming to the party. *You must be joking, Mrs. Poley?* I kid you not. *Well, I suppose it's none of my business.* Correct. *But let me tell you, that dog of yours—* Excuse me, it's not my dog—*I don't care whose dog it is, Mrs. Poley, it shouldn't be there and I consider it my business! What about public health?* Well, what about it? Dead birds lie around for days, mauled by cats. I have seen separate heads and tails of lizards everywhere. Pieces of mouse. Half a squirrel. The earth, in its mysterious way, absorbs. Nature takes care.

After a silence, hostility takes over again. Mrs. Cody finds herself in a world she doesn't understand. Therefore it is wrong. It is dangerous. She lowers her white flag, which has been fluttering uncertainly for months, anyway,

and goes over the top. I am seen in my true colors; a
threat; I lower the tone of the neighborhood. On this Eve
of peace on earth and goodwill toward men, we are
enemies. Mrs. Cody doesn't say this, but I hear it. She
will have several phone calls to make tonight. *Just wait till
I tell you what Mrs. Poley's done now! There's been a lot
of strange comings and goings in that house, I should say,
and I've minded my business because they've never been
noisy about it, but this is enough to provoke a saint! Mrs.
Poley is sitting alone in her house with somebody else's
dead dog on the steps outside. Can you imagine? Can you
conceive of the state of mind of a woman like that?*

DECEMBER 25th

A LONG, UNPREMEDITATED NAP and another Sahara dream: slow, uphill walk to a hotel perched on a pyramid of dunes and fringed by cool, tall palms. No other place to stay, my guide explained as we trudged up the dusty, slanting wall of sand against a tide of other people streaming easily, joyfully down. I leaped from the couch when the phone rang.

Mrs. Poley! I hate to trouble you at this hour, and I know you're not—well, you've got problems—but your sprinklers are still sprinkling! You are flooding the street! A river is flowing into my carport! D'you want to wash us away in our beds? (Yes.) PLEASE TURN OFF YOUR SPRINKLERS, *Mrs. Poley! Thank you and Merry Christmas.*

Sorry about that. What time is it? One o'clock? I'll be jiggered. God rest you merry, Mrs. Cody.

Most of the canyon lights are switched off now. A dog barks somewhere, as usual encouraging others. When they stop, there's a beautiful silence, followed by the sound of an approaching car, grotesquely loud. I half-expect vague snatches of song from homecoming revelers. But the car stops outside my door and is a Yellow Cab. The driver gets out, removes two large suitcases from the trunk, dumps them gingerly on the soaking sidewalk. He holds open the passenger door and a woman emerges. From inside, I switch on a bluish floodlight. It picks up dog first, of course, then an unknown person who has obviously made a mistake. All the same, she waves at the driver to carry her luggage and heads up the steps. Both are surprised by dog, to say nothing of cascading puddles, but press on firmly to my porch.

Opening door, I confront a slightly exotic old lady with a burned skin and jet-black hair. Something of the buzzard in her heavy-lidded eyes, reconnoitering me with a hopeful glare, in the clawlike hand that grips an airlines bag, in the wizened but alert manner that she seems to hover rather than stand. She says I must be Dora. Now I strip her mentally of light tweed suit under transparent plastic raincoat and garland her with pink feathers.

"My God. Won't you come in?"

She looks surprised. "I flew a thousand miles and brought my luggage, so I wasn't planning to stay outside." Speaks with no trace of foreign accent, though I'm not sure whether I expected Big-Chief-Pony-That-Walks stuff, anyway. A Southwestern flatness, with no burr in it, and a hint of backwoods that I hear echoed in Keith.

Entering the living room, Malowaka asks: "Where's Skippy?", which turns out to be her grandson's nickname. She's surprised I never heard it. "Back home, he's just Skippy." I reply that he's out at the moment, and she doesn't ask me to explain this right away, having explanations of her own to give first. Taking off raincoat, perching on arm of chair like bird in its aerie, she opens the airlines bag, brings out a pack of cheroots, offers me one, which I refuse, and lights up. Wreathed in pungent smoke, she tells me she decided to surprise her grandson by spending Christmas with him. Her daughter and son-in-law invited her over to Montrose for the holidays, but no thank you. Too much trouble and carrying on around there, she wants a good time. That's why she thought, Skippy! Tried to telephone in advance, but all the lines were busy. People are always calling people around Christmas, it's one hell of a nuisance. Would like a cup of hot coffee, please, with a jigger of Scotch in it. Pretty little house, by the way. Hopes, chuckling, there's a spare room. If not, will roll up in a blanket on the couch. Pokes upholstery with a claw, pronounces it comfortable. Now how about that coffee? She'll come into the kitchen and talk to me while I make it.

Getting up, she looks around, takes her bearings and reaches the kitchen before I do. As I fill the kettle with water, she frowns and asks if I don't have an electric pot. They're much better; if she'd known, she'd have brought us one for Christmas. Is giving us a Broilitzer, by the way —in the brown suitcase, that's why it's so heavy. Do I know about these? Lovely little electric broilers with a bell that rings when the steak is done rare, medium or well. They broil the best steak she ever tasted. I promise to look into electric pots, then ask politely about her trip.

"Good. I like planes, they're quick, people look after you, make a good cup of coffee."

Then she gives me a shrewd, darting, expectant look. I feel the moment has come.

"Malowaka . . . may I call you that?"

"It's my name, honey. Got no other."

"Keith isn't here because we've separated."

She asks simply, without comment or commiseration: "Then where is he?"

"Staying with friends in Hollywood. I've got the number, would you like me to call for you?"

She asks if Hollywood is far away. About twelve miles, I tell her, and she whistles with surprise, exclaims how expensive the taxi will be. So I offer to drive her. "That's good of you, honey. Try the number."

No one answers.

"I suppose they're out at a party. They'll probably be back soon."

She laughs. "In a pig's eye. He always liked to sit up half the night. Water's boiling."

I fold a filter paper and place it in the glass funnel of my coffeemaker. Malowaka watches. "They make good coffee too, but they're slow." Taps my refrigerator, opens and closes door of my stove. "You like gas? I got both, because I can't make up my mind which I like better. Electric's slow, but cleaner." Reminds me to put the Scotch in her coffee, and we go back to the living room. She settles on the couch this time, putting her feet up, takes a sip of coffee and approves.

"Now, before you tell me about Skippy, tell me about what's going on outside. Everything's wet, and there's a dead dog."

"I know. I'm sorry about that, Malowaka." Her matter-of-factness makes me smile; also reduces the situation to a kind of farce, as if I'm a sloppy housewife. I explain the problem with the law and she says: "There's cops for you. Never had any time for them myself. You got to tell them where they get off, believe you me. Now, what happened with you and Skippy?"

"You're sure you're not tired? It's after one o'clock."

"I won't sleep yet, honey. Coffee keeps me awake." She compliments me on the house again. "Never been in California before, and it's dark so I can't see a thing, but it looks nice. Is it serious? Are you going to get a divorce?"

"We haven't discussed it yet. I suppose so."

"He leave you or you leave him?"

"The former."

"What?"

"Keith left me, four days ago."

"It figures. The men in our family always leave their wives."

"Why is that, do you think, Malowaka?"

She laughs, coughs, spits out a piece of loose tobacco from the cheroot. "No offense, honey, but if you'd seen the wives, you'd understand. Where are you *from* that makes you talk that way?"

"England."

A vague but impressed stare. "You must have come a long way. Longer than I've come?"

"Oh yes."

"Much longer?"

"Let me see. About six times as far, I'd say."

She whistles. "That's far. I don't know much about where's where. Never been anywhere. There's a lot of things I never bother with. Newspapers! If it's important, you get it on the radio. I got it about Medicare on the radio, took sick at once, went to a hospital for free. They weren't kidding. Now, if Skippy left you, who gets the house?"

"It belongs to me."

"How's that?" She shoots this out at me. "You sign papers?"

"No. Keith didn't want a house, you see, but agreed to let me buy one."

"But did you sign papers, honey?"

"For the house?"

"Property settlement."

"We never bothered."

"You better look into that right away. My cousin Charley walked out on his wife last year. It was her mother's house, but when she sold it, he got half." Another darting look. "But maybe Skippy'll change his mind, come back to you?"

"It doesn't look like it, I'm afraid."

"Well, I like the way you're handling this." She gave me a direct, approving stare. "If you were Lucy—that's my daughter—you'd be howling and screaming." She laughed heartily at the thought. "You'd be bawling your head off, or falling down dead drunk outside my door. How about calling that number again, and seeing if my boy's come home?"

I obeyed instantly, and again there was no answer.

"So he's making a night of it." She laughed at this, too. "That's my Skippy."

"You're welcome to the spare room, of course."

"Yeah. Now why did he walk out on a pretty house and a pretty girl like you?"

"Oh. Well . . . That's so hard to explain, Malowaka."

She shook her head. "A thing like that, it's always simple. Another girl?" I denied it, and she looked astonished. "You sure? You sure there's no other girl you just don't know about?"

"It's more complicated than that. Excuse me. I hardly know you—I like you very much, let me say that at once—but it really is a complicated situation and I don't know whether I can simply _plunge in_. Besides, it may take hours."

"I got time." Sipped her coffee. "I want to get it straightened out. If he's not coming back to you, he'll be coming back to me. I got to know about that. If he's coming back to me, you see, I got to call Silly. Silly's a fellow works for me around the house. I call him Silly because he's like a girl. Knows how to make good coffee and broil a steak, though."

After a moment, I burst out laughing. Malowaka laughed too, almost choked with it, tears streaming down her face. "Hadn't thought it was as funny as that, honey. But when you think about it, it's the funniest thing I ever heard."

I stared at her. "What?"

"Calling him Silly." She laughed again, then wiped her eyes.

"You're a fantastically pragmatic woman."

"What?"

I'd said this involuntarily, and the moment I'd done so, knew she wouldn't understand.

"It's a way of . . ." I gave up. "Nothing."

"Now listen, I'd like you to explain that word. If that's what I am, I better know about it."

"Well . . . Pragmatic means practical."

She looked disappointed. "That all?"

"Not exactly. It implies a point of view. It's the way you go about things. For instance—oh, this is difficult!—imagine a person faced with a certain situation. Imagine you're a woman whose husband just left you."

"Mine died."

"Good."

"What?"

"I mean that's a good example. One type of person can't really accept a death. She goes over and over in her mind about how unfair or unnecessary or whose fault it was. She wonders about death itself. Is there a next world, will she ever see him again? Or is life all there is, and if so, how can it possibly be lived without him?" Saw I was losing her. She gave a quick, impatient munch on her cheroot. "In other words, she gets hung up over the whole shebang." Malowaka brightened and nodded. "But the other type—and that's *you*—the other type just says, okay, he's dead, that's it, what's next and where do I find it?"

"Sure. You got to make sense about a thing like that."

"It's not always easy."

She chuckled. "Not always easy to die, honey. So Skippy fools around, that's your problem?"

"I didn't say that."

"You going to say it now?"

"Well . . . It's part of the problem. I don't believe,

you see, that anybody should keep anybody on a string. But somehow, Keith thinks I do. He thinks I object, when I don't. In spite of everything, he feels guilty, and he can't bear that, so he gets angry with me for making him feel guilty. And the whole point is, I'm really begging him to feel okay."

Malowaka brooded on this, then said in a slightly offended voice: "I wasn't born yesterday."

"I'm certainly aware of that."

"Somebody's all wet. Skippy fools around and you don't mind, but I bet *you* don't fool around?"

"That's true, but——"

"If he does it, why can't you?"

"I don't happen to want to."

"Then no wonder Skippy feels bad." Her tone was positively accusing. "If you play it that way, you don't play it fair. He's out having a good time, but you stay home and watch TV or something. Well, you'll make any man feel bad, honey, if you go on like that. My cousin Charley always quarreled with his wife about where they'd go for a vacation. She wanted Hawaii, he wanted—I can't remember, some place else. Anyway, I tell them, stop arguing and go to *both*, otherwise one of you has a bad time while the other's having a good one." Shrugged. "They wouldn't listen. So one gives in and the other walks out."

"I'm afraid that analogy doesn't quite hold."

"You got another long word to explain."

"I'm sorry. I mean, you make it sound too simple."

Her chin went up and her eyes glared, friendly but defiant. "Knock it down if you can."

"That involves telling you a lot of things, Malowaka, and I'm not sure if I can. I hardly know you."

"I don't know *you*, but I speak my mind."

"But you're only asking the questions. I've got to give the answers. I'm not the sort of person who can tell just anybody the intimate details of my marriage. Not that you're anybody, but you come in out of the night, from a different background and a different culture . . ." Malowaka's eyelids drooped. I was losing her again. "Oh, what the hell. Keith fools around, but it's with more than one person at a time."

"You'd like it better if there was only one? You're crazy, honey. If there was only one, it might be serious."

"You never let me finish a point." Suddenly impatient with her for joining the ranks of all those who put me in the wrong, I decided to take the plunge. "It's more than one person, but *all at the same time!*"

She watched me with a puzzled, groping expression. Then her face cleared. "You mean, like kids at school?"

"I don't think I mean that at all."

"It sounds like you do. Kids get together by themselves and find out what it's all about." She chuckled. "Skippy's always had a bit of the kid left in him. Sometimes they don't grow up all the way—didn't anybody teach you that, where you came from?"

"Well, suppose you're right." *Just enough truth in your annoying folk wisdom, you old buzzard, to force me to speak out.* "What can I do? They play records and talk for hours. It's like parties where people won't go home and are still there but nowhere when dawn comes up. I can't live that way. It wastes too much time."

"You got some more Scotch?"

"Plenty. Why don't I just fetch the bottle?"

"Fix yourself a shot of something, too. It'll help you relax."

In the kitchen, paused to try and realign myself; couldn't make up my mind whether I was more fascinated than indignant; in any case, saw no way out of the following situation. My absent husband's Ute grandmother, born in a wickiup, raised in tremendous poverty, roots for breakfast and so on, a creature of natural cunning and acquired riches, had invaded my house and was preparing to take over my life. I was expected to drink my way into Christmas morn at her side. _What were her motives?_ Was she, in her shrewdly primitive way, casting herself in the role of Mrs. Fix-It? Or was she bent on taking her favorite drinking companion back to the reservation? Unable to answer yet, I decided on red wine with a roach, took one from a mock-Victorian kitchen jar labeled MARIHUANA and returned to the living room with bottles of wine and Scotch.

Malowaka had removed an envelope of photographs from her airlines bag, and was shuffling them. "Come and look at these, honey." More King-of-the-Mountain snapshots of the old lady surrounded by a crew of oil-riggers, proudly extending a claw streaked with the rich grease, posed beneath a derrick and somehow not dwarfed at all by its looming pyramid. I congratulated her and asked if she'd care to join me in a little pot.

She shook her head. "Skippy used to try that stuff on me, but I get too excited. I'll stick to Scotch."

Sitting in a chair, tucking in my feet, trying to make

myself as comfortable as my guest, I took a drag and a swallow of wine. "People accuse me of being a puritan," I said, "because I like to keep my relationships personal and approach them with the idea that they may be lasting." Received a blank, discouraging stare. "Do you understand, or am I being too general again?"

"I don't know what you're being, honey. Try it another way, and I'll tell you whether it makes sense or not. Keep it simple, too."

"Not to mince matters, you can call me as horny as the next girl. Or boy. But if I like someone, and he likes me, I prefer to find him there when I wake up in the morning."

"Somebody's all wet. If you want to keep them, why do you lose them?"

"Malowaka, you have an extraordinary way of turning everything I say against me."

She looked pleased. "Is that so? I appreciate the way you're handling this, believe you me, I like it that you don't howl and scream, but Skippy got the point better than you."

I stared at her. "What point?"

"He wrote me he was going to marry you and invited me to the wedding. I couldn't make it because I caught the darned flu. Had to stay in bed with Silly fussing around, until he caught it, too. Anyway, I called Skippy and asked him, you sure you want to get married? Well, he said, I met this girl who certainly wants to marry *me*, and that's never happened before."

"Really? Keith said that?"

"Sure. Then I asked him, what's she like, this girl

who's trying to get you, and he said—we got nothing in common, Granny, and that's why I feel good."

"He said that, too?"

"Sure. I seen too many people who get married, he said, because they think they're right for each other. Get married knowing you're wrong, and maybe all hell won't break loose after all. It sounded to me Skippy knew his business, so I told him fine, go ahead, see what happens."

"It's the most cold-blooded thing I ever heard. From both of you! No wonder I felt like a guinea pig. I was a mere experiment, I was being tried on for size."

"So why d'you marry Skippy, then?"

Before answering, took a long drag; held it in for a long while, wondering how to convey to Malowaka, in simple terms, an experience so tangled and unresolved. Began by venturing to comment that, just as her own truths were too simple, so, contrariwise, a platitude may contain part of a truth. (She poured herself a double.) You look at someone and feel a lively desire to be better strangers. Not just sexual attraction, which may not even be strong at first, but the sense of an answer waiting, a secret ready to be confided. That six-day drive across America was a journey intended to obliterate my own past. I saw Keith as a figure out of the future, stepped directly from that new landscape. The wandering bark, after years at sea, thought it had found its star.

Malowaka gave an approving nod. "You mean you tried Skippy out, too. So what's the difference?"

"But——"

"There isn't any. And nothing wrong with it, neither. I told Charley when he was arguing with his wife about

97

a vacation—if *she* wants to, I said, you go there. If you don't like it, tell her to start packing. You quit a place you don't like, but you got to see it first."

"You're really incredibly alike, you and Keith."

"We get along."

"I see now where it comes from, his way of looking at something, thinking maybe it's what I need, let's try it and see. I suppose——"

Without warning, Malowaka keeled over and lay flat on her back on the couch. I leaped up in alarm, but she dangled a claw and murmured: "It's okay, I had a long trip and I'm flaking out." Decisive to the last, she plummeted at once into sleep. I put a blanket over her. Propped against a pillow, her head looked like a mask on a totem pole. Airlines bag was on the arm of the couch, photographs peeping out; two large suitcases, one heavy with Broilitzer, stood like watchdogs by the front door. Although disturbed and exhausted by our strange encounter, I felt a wave of fellow-feeling. We were both exiles; had come, as Malowaka said, from a long way. She breathed loudly in her sleep, and I wondered about her struggle, death of a husband when she was forty, loneliness at eighty of tent, Silly, no one to love except her distant Keith. How did she survive? As this question occurred, she made a dreadful pig-noise; snorted, gobbled and gasped; and subsided again into peace.

Unlike Malowaka, I'd be awake for hours. Sitting down opposite her, I picked up a book. *Every exception tends to disappear and to return to the rule. Exceptions are snares, and we ought above all to distrust them when they charm our vanity. To catch and fix a fickle heart is*

*a task which tempts all women; and a man finds some-
thing intoxicating in the tears of tenderness and joy which
he alone has had the power to draw from a proud woman.
But attractions of this kind are deceptive. Affinity of
nature is the only affinity which is worth anything. The
being we love must not be mysterious and sphinx-like,
but clear and limpid as a diamond; so that admiration
and attachment may grow with knowledge.* What did he
know about it? Never took the plunge. Sat around in
Switzerland, where nothing ever happens, touting melancholy grandeur.

Threw Amiel to the floor, rose and switched off garden
floodlight, leaving dog to darkness. Retired to my room,
where Malowaka also awaited me, feathered and gloating
on the wall.

Having retrieved Amiel, lain in bed for two hours
reading him, become reconciled, found his *weltschmerz*
rather endearing after all, I slept and woke at my usual
hour of nine o'clock. On my lips, a remembered phrase,
*One single black speck may be the beginning of a gan-
grene, of a storm, of a revolution*; which I found puzzling,
until I connected it to a passage in which the diarist remarked that a single point of departure can decide the
whole future of an existence; which I found grim. Faced
the day in spite of this, crossed my living room (Malowaka still out on couch, dog still out on steps), entered
my kitchen and prepared breakfast tea. Sipping, I dialed
a number on the phone.

"Good morning, Keith. Merry Christmas. Your
Granny's here."

A dazed and sleepy exclamation.

"It's true. She turned up in the middle of the night, hoping to surprise you. I explained we were living apart, then tried to reach you, but you were out. We had a long talk. I find her quite remarkable. She's still asleep, but will be stirring shortly, I imagine. What would you like me to do with her?"

"She ought to have called before she took off."

"She tried. The lines were busy."

"Well, I don't want her up here now. I need more sleep."

"So?"

"Listen, I'm coming to your party, so tell her you couldn't reach me this morning, I stayed the night in Long Beach, I'll be back this afternoon and see her later."

"You expect me to take her out to lunch?"

"I thought you were enjoying her."

"In a way."

"What did you talk about?"

"You, of course."

"Okay. See you later. I'll come early, soon as I can put all my pieces together. And thank you, Dora." Hung up without wishing me compliments of the season, forgivable because I'd woken him up with alarming news. Also, he sounded depressed. Or was it just another hangover? Keith never greeted the day with enthusiasm, so it was difficult to tell.

I moved to switch on the radio, but the phone rang.

"Merry Christmas, girl."

"Oh, Merry Christmas, Octavia."

"How's the situation?"

"Greg didn't call back. The old couple's visiting relatives, I suppose. Nice thing to come home to."

"I'd rather come home to it than live with it. Are you still very hung up this morning?"

"Oddly enough, I felt almost fatalistic when I saw it first thing. It seemed a kind of a fixture. Partly due to rigor mortis, no doubt. Anyway, I've got something else on my mind—and my hands. The grandmother's here."

"Keith's? You poor angel. Who needs it?"

"Yes, that's rather my feeling."

"But why don't you just send her up to the Prells, C.O.D.?"

"He doesn't wish it. Wishes to sleep. Is coming over early this afternoon. What did you do last night?"

"There was a party. Friends of the Prells, even higher, and I mean higher, up in the hills than they are."

"Well, I'm not sorry to have missed that."

A pause, then Octavia said in a quiet, matter-of-fact tone: "Mark walked out on Rosemary and me."

"At the party? How? And why?"

"Simply said he couldn't stand the situation any more. Told Rosemary she had to decide. Rosemary played it very cool, said not on Christmas Eve. So he walked out and no one knows where he is."

"Then it's just you and her and Andy now?"

"That's right. Maybe *we*'ll come over early too. Would you like that?"

"Yes, I think so."

"What time?"

"I shall have to feed the grandmother first, but I'll be back by three-thirty."

"You can probably use a little help getting things ready, anyway."

"I hadn't really thought about it. I've made no preparations at all."

"You must have bought the food?"

"No. I've done nothing. There's booze, of course, but under the circumstances I'm damned if I'm going to cook. I'll find a delicatessen that's open today, buy a turkey and lots of that depressing potato salad they put in cartons. I shall serve everything on carboard plates. If possible, with disposable plastic knives and forks. And Dixie cups for the liquor."

"Don't forget your paper napkins. They come with floral patterns now."

"Good."

"You're determined to make it that horrible?"

"I don't care. But it's less trouble to make things horrible. After all, it's Keith's party. I only asked Chad."

"Why?"

"Because I have no friends."

"Oh, come on, Dora."

"It's true. Apart from you and Chad, no real friends. The rest are all those people who love me, and whom I hardly know."

"You're feeling better, I can tell. There's a healthy mean streak coming out."

"Yes. If no one claims that dog today, I may put a rose between its teeth."

As I came back to the living room, grandmother snorted and woke. Bewildered at first to find herself in a strange house, on a couch, fully dressed, she had a quick recall, looked out of the window and admired the ocean. "Look at that. Isn't it beautiful? Merry Christmas, honey. Why don't you call Skippy?"

I repeated Keith's lie and promise for him, then suggested she might care to clean up and change. Carried a suitcase to the spare room, after being instructed to leave the one containing Broilitzer where it was, and getting no hint as to what she intended doing with it. When I asked how she felt about breakfast or lunch, she replied, did I mean dinner? There would be turkey this evening, I explained, when the guests arrived, but in the meantime I'd be happy to take her somewhere, depending on what she fancied. Malowaka fancied, immediately, pancakes. Silly had been in Los Angeles, told her the pancakes were the best thing in it, came back raving about them, described dozens of places that specialized in dozens of different kinds.

"I think you mean that chain called Aunt Clara's Pancake Kitchen, and there's one in Santa Monica. I'll find out if it's open."

Malowaka prepared to shower and I dialed a number.

"Hello, my name is Frances!" said a voice at the other end of the line. "Can I help you?"

"You're open today, I presume?"

"We certainly are! There's a Christmas Special, turkey, home-baked mince pie, coffee, tea or milk, choice of soup or salad."

"But are there pancakes too?"

"Sure thing." Frances sounded surprised. "It's our specialty, you know."

From the outside, Aunt Clara's was a gingerbreadish house with pink gables, diamond windowpanes and a canary-yellow front door. Inside, low rafters and checkered tablecloths created a beerhall atmosphere. No liquor license, however; tables were packed with families apparently pleased to celebrate the season with coffee, tea or milk. A Christmas tree winked colored lights. Carols, orchestrated as richly as Viennese waltzes, were piped in. Malowaka had dressed up considerably for our outing, touch of rouge on bony cheeks, though no lipstick, brightly flowered dress with a flared "peasant" skirt, scarlet cardigan worn over her shoulders and row of heavy silver bangles on her left wrist. In trousers, turtleneck sweater and no makeup except the usual touch of eyeshadow, I felt moderately sluttish at her side.

Picking up a menu the size of a newspaper, Malowaka whistled with approval. "They got everything here, buckwheat, potato, apple, chicken, blue cheese, boysenberry, German and Swedish. Silly knew what he was talking about for once in his life."

A waitress came up in baby-blue uniform, swinging an order pad attached by a chain to her waist. She was tiny but gave herself inches with high heels and bouffant hair; her pretty, friendly face, painted as bright as a doll's, suggested she'd been born smiling. "Hello!" Voice had a slight Southern drawl. "My name is Dora." Pointed to a button on her lapel which confirmed it. "Can I help you?"

"I'll be darned. My name is Dora too."

Her smile remained broad, but her eyes flickered uncertainly. "You're not putting me on, are you? We have to do it this way, it's a rule of the management."

"My name is Dora, I promise you. Hello."

"Hello!" Pause. "You're English, aren't you?"

I nodded. "You better believe it."

"Isn't that something?"

"Are you Southern?"

"I'm from Monroe, Louisiana. You want coffee now on the turkey dinner?"

"No turkey," Malowaka said. "Pancakes."

"This," I told Dora, "is my mother-in-law."

The smile hesitated. "Really? Now where's she from?"

"I'm not English," Malowaka said.

"She's American Indian, Dora."

"Hello!" Dora said to Malowaka. "What kind of pancake do you want?"

"Three kinds." She listed buttermilk, chicken, pineapple, side-order of sausage patty, French toast.

"Coffee now?"

"Now." Note of impatience in the grandmother's tone.

"I think I'll just have breakfast, Dora. Scrambled eggs and bacon, tea."

She scribbled this down. "Not very Christmasy, is it? We got eggnog if you want."

"Christmas comes later for me, if at all."

"Do *I* know how you feel?" She laughed, responding to this with disconcerting enthusiasm. "It's not going to come at all for me this year." Gave me a sharp, knowing look, imagining my savage drama with full-blooded American Indian husband, assuming that *I* imagined, in her case, serious boyfriend trouble.

"Toast?"

"No thank you."

"You're right. It's the worst, especially if you're crazy about it. Imagine, I can put on pounds, just on toast and butter and jelly."

"Do you mind working Christmas Day, Dora?"

"You get double pay. And it's good for the figure and keeps me out of mischief." She went off, little body swaying on high heels, for Malowaka's coffee.

There we are, I thought; two unsolved mysteries for each other. I'd never know why she wanted to work Christmas Day. She'd never discover why I sat here with Malowaka, who now remarked she was afraid she'd never get her coffee, let alone her pancakes, Dora and I were talking up such a storm.

"Oh, it was enjoyable," I said.

"Why?"

As a rule I don't enter into conversations with strangers; especially if, to use a dreadful phrase, they are ordinary people. This is not superiority, but defensiveness; feel I have nothing to offer them; they do their job, let me do mine. Always discourage the nuisance who strikes up eager, meaningless conversations at bus stop or any waiting line, the cabdriver, the plumber or man who comes to read one's gas meter and wishes to discuss politics, gardens, teenagers. These people will talk to anybody, and I find it insulting.

"I really don't know, Malowaka. I suppose because we have the same name."

Dora returned with Malowaka's coffee, gave me a conspiratorial wink and went off again.

"Silly told me people are kind of friendly out here. Guess he was right for the second time in his life." Malowaka suddenly clasped my hand. "You've been real friendly, I want you to know I appreciate it."

"I *feel* friendly toward you, my dear."

"And I want to tell you again, I like the way you're handling this. Sometimes I don't get exactly what you're about, sometimes you talk pretty funny, but I can see why Skippy picked on you." *Last night the old buzzard told me I picked on Skippy; but leave it alone.* "I'm going to tell him when I see him."

"Well, thank you. I feel resigned and peaceful in a hopeless sort of way this Christmas morn. I realize it's not enough and has got me precisely nowhere, but I feel I've said my say and done what I can do."

She seemed disappointed. "You don't want to go on talking about it?"

"Not really. Also, I took a tranquilizer."

Her spirits and interest revived. "What kind d'you take?"

"Librium. You know it? A little green and black capsule."

"They give me Miltown, just plain white."

"It makes me sleepy. Librium keeps me alert but soothed. But why are you on Miltown, Malowaka?"

"I'm not, right now. Doctor tells me to go easy on it when I'm on Scotch." There was something apologetic in her smile. "You should see me act bad up there. I tell Silly to get the hell out, can't stand you swishing around a minute longer, I tell him, get the hell out. I call up Lucy long distance, just to bother her. How are you, I tell her, are you on the sauce, throwing a tantrum or locking him out of the house this week? I get moods.

Can't stand anybody, anything. That's when I go off liquor for a couple of days and take Miltown."

I patted her hand. It had gone unexpectedly limp. "You get lonely up there, I'm sure."

"Well, I got no one to talk to."

"Aren't there other of your—other people on the reservation?"

"You got neighbors too, haven't you?"

I smiled. The eyes glared at me, haunted as well as passionate. The hand recovered its strength, gripping my wrist tightly. The mouth opened, preparing for speech, and snapped shut again, as if thinking better of it. Then the face leaned close to mine.

"Listen, Skippy called me on the phone last month and said Granny, I got a great idea. You should come out here. Live with Dora and me."

"Really? He never mentioned it."

"I came out last night hoping to surprise him, but I thought maybe he'd ask me to stay as well. Guess it won't happen now. Not just on account of you and him, but . . ." The heavy lids drooped and twitched. "Looks like it was just an idea, anyway. Why didn't he hurry back from Long Beach when he heard I was come?"

Confessing a wound, she was inflicting another, at the same time, on her pride. This love of Keith was fanatical but touching. "He doesn't know you're here, Malowaka. Remember, I only spoke to someone at the house where he's staying. They didn't have the number in Long Beach, otherwise we'd have called him."

Dora arrived with a heap of plates, one for me and

four for Malowaka. Appeased by my explanation, surrounded by food, the grandmother brightened, attack-
ing her pancakes and side-orders, pronouncing everything
good. Delight kept her silent for a while, during which I
remembered that Keith had once mentioned casually the
idea of asking Malowaka to share our house. It must have
been at least three months ago. I responded with cautious
enthusiasm, saying I'd rather not have her in the house
itself, but perhaps we might convert the carport into a
little guest apartment. He reacted unfavorably. "If you
want to make plans and all that shit, it's no good. If she
could just come here, simply, no sweat, see how she likes
it, is all I meant." The subject was not brought up again,
and I didn't think about it. Should have, obviously; saw
now that a move in Malowaka's direction was a move
away from me; understood Keith's confusion when I'd
told him a few hours ago that she was here, waiting for
him. Malowaka would force the issue. Seeing her, Keith
would wonder instantly if she wasn't, after all, what he
needed. He would taste the prospect of waking up in the
morning to drink her coffee and gaze at mountains, forgetting the previous day, which had no longer happened,
because he'd never really wanted it to.

Peacefulness and resignation, which I'd exaggerated
anyway, flew off like startled birds. I saw that everything
would be decided very soon; saw Malowaka, facing me
across the table, as an unfavorable card turned up in my
private Tarot pack. She finished her enormous meal,
wiped her mouth with a paper napkin, took out a cheroot.
I struck a match.

After the silence, and our moment of closeness, we seemed to be looking each other over.

"I think," I said, "I'd like one too."

She grinned, handed me a cheroot and lit it for me. We sat twined in smoke, incurring glances of surprise and disapproval.

Malowaka walked briskly ahead while I carried shopping bag up steps, past dog. I stopped because it looked ghastly again; single black speck under a blue sky and mellow sun. I imagined a photograph of the scene. Years pass, and the snapshot reposes in an album. One sees Dora Poley in sweater and trousers, clutching turkey and cartons of potato salad, standing on her steps, dead dog at her feet. She looks toward ocean and frowns with alarm. In the background, Malowaka waits and smiles. _Christmas Day, Santa Monica, California._

Wrapped in transparent plastic paper, glazed and frilled, dead bird is set on platter. Potato salad chills in refrigerator. Malowaka takes a nap. Phone rings and I turn down radio, playing "Cherish."

"Dora?"

A voice that I recognize but cannot place. Other voices behind it: chink of glasses, laughter, and the same station playing "Cherish."

"Richard!"

"Oh God."

"That's quite a reaction."

"I'm sorry. It wasn't horror, just surprise. I'm always thrown by a voice from the past out of the blue."

"I had an impulse to call you and wish you Merry Christmas."

"How very sweet. Thank you. Merry Christmas. How are you? At a party, by the sound of it."

"Yes. I'm fine. And the good news finally broke last week."

"What?"

"I've got a movie, Dora. A real part in a real movie!"

"How wonderful. I'm thrilled."

"So am I. And I thought of you when it happened. Wanted to call you right away, tell you I wished you'd been around, then, there, at that moment. I thought how unfair we had ten months together when everything was bad. Then I decided to wait till Christmas, call you up and tell you then."

"How very sweet."

"You were so patient. I was so impossible."

"I . . ."

"You all right?"

"No."

"What's the matter?"

"Let it go."

"What? You're still married, aren't you?"

"I'm not sure."

"That's a shame."

"Yes. Richard, where are you? Can I have your number? I might call you later."

A moment of hesitation. "Well, we're kind of moving around all day, going to a couple more parties. You know how it is. But I'll give you my home number, if you like. You could try me tomorrow. Oh, wait a minute, I'll be at the studio, got a wardrobe fitting. Still . . ." He gave me the number. I didn't write it down. "You could try me in the afternoon, I may be through by then."

"Thank you, Richard. And thank you for calling me. I'm thrilled about the part. Merry Christmas."

"Merry Christmas, Dora. Nice talking to you. Take care now."

Up yours.

Bottles and Dixie cups on living room chest. Long Mexican dining table covered with vinyl rose-pattern cloth, exquisitely drugstore, green paper napkins, blue cardboard plates. Malowaka still naps. Phone rings and I turn down radio, playing "A Groovy Kind of Love."

Beep-beep, then a brisk operator's voice: "Is this Gladstone 8-6647?"

"Yes."

"Is this Miss Penny Skiles?"

"No."

"Hold the line, please." Mutter of conversation, then a man says: "Excuse me. Try Fell. Ask for Octavia Fell."

"Is this Miss Octavia Fell?"

"No. She'll be here in about an hour, probably."

"Hold the line, please." Another round of mutters, and the man says: "Okay, operator, that's fine."

"Are you there?"

"Yes."

"When Miss Fell arrives, please ask her to call Operator four fifty-four, long distance."

"All right. Who's trying to reach her?"

"Mr. Skiles, calling from Toronto."

*So Father remembers Christmas as well as birthdays.
Also, in spite of what she says, Octavia wants him to call.
Otherwise, why leave word where she is? Interesting!
And her real name's Penny Skiles.*

This time, when I turn it down, radio's playing "Like
a Rolling Stone."

"Hello, could I speak to Mrs. Poley?" English voice,
male and totally unfamiliar.

"Speaking."

"We haven't actually met but I believe you've heard
about me. My name's Mark Cusden."

"Yes. You're a friend of Jim and Andy and Octavia
and Rosemary."

"Well, Rosemary mainly."

"None of them's here, I'm afraid."

"But you're expecting them, aren't you?"

"I'm expecting everybody. Would you like to come
too?"

"No thanks. Terribly kind of you, all the same."
Nervous laugh. "Look, this is a bit tricky, and you're
probably much too busy right now——"

"Not at all. I have nothing to do but wait. And I'm
rather enjoying these unexpected phone calls, now I've
got the hang of them. Octavia already told me, by the
way, about what happened last night. So please tell me
more, if you like."

"Yes, well. Good. You're English too?"

"Yes."

"Lived here long?"

"Less than two years."

"I was here in fifty-six for a while, then took off. I came _back_, quite recently, and met Rosemary through some friends at the beach. Well. You've heard what's been going on, I suppose?"

"I believe I'm in the general picture, and I suppose you more or less know about _me_."

"Yes. Sorry about all that. Anyway, the point is, I've thought it over and decided to take off again."

"Really? Where?"

"Well, back where I came from."

"England? You can't be serious."

"Good God, no. I've been living in Nukuhiva—that's a sort of island in the South Pacific, very tiny, practically nothing to it, but beautiful. Lots of sun. I came back here with this friend of mine, just on a trip. Then . . . do you _really_ mind my telling you this? I'd absolutely understand if you'd rather not."

"I'd rather. We're not total strangers, after all, even though we've never met."

"That's true. Wheels within wheels." He laughs again. There's a breezy, schoolboyish quality in Mark. No matter what he talks about, it sounds simple and all in the day's work. "Know what I mean?"

"Yes, so please go on and don't be embarrassed. I'm not a conventional person."

"I gathered that."

"Really? I'm glad."

"Yes. Anyway, I went to look up some old friends, and met Rosemary. It looked pretty serious for a while. I even thought of staying on, not going back."

"What about your friend from Nukuhiva?"

"Bit of a problem there, of course."

"I can imagine."

"Thunder on the left _and_ the right, in fact." Another laugh. "So it all got too complicated. Rosemary runs with a complicated crowd. I began to feel depressed and a bit disgusted with the whole thing, so I'm taking off again."

"I have a feeling you made the right decision."

"Thanks. Anyway, I called your house on the off-chance they might all be there and I'd say good-by, but I'm rather glad now they're not."

"I'll tell them, if you like. When are you leaving?"

"Tonight. My friend just got the tickets."

"How enviable. You'll be in the South Seas tomorrow."

"Well, it's a bit confusing, because of the International Date Line, and the roundabout way you get there—we fly to Papeete, then take a boat—so we won't _actually_ be _back_ in Nukuhiva for, oh, I'd say at least four days."

"It sounds wonderful, all the same—lagoons and long white beaches and eternal sun."

"Yes, I love the sun. So please tell everyone I called."

"Indeed I will. _Bon voyage_."

"Thanks. I'm quite sorry we never actually met."

"Maybe we will—somewhere, some day, before we're both old and gray."

"Don't think about that." Laughs again. "Good-by."

The International Date Line: I'd say we've all crossed it.

Racing-green Dodge parks behind my yellow and black Ghia. Three people get out, Andy and Octavia and a girl who must be Rosemary. The sudden concentration of color is dazzling, Octavia in purple jacket and trousers, Andy wearing a tangerine sweater. From a distance, Rosemary is long gold hair, tight suede pants of the same shade, and a split-level sweater, scarlet on one side, white on the other. As if it's a famous landmark, Octavia points out dog. They follow her up the steps. From the threshold, Rosemary is a pair of beautiful gray eyes, staring into mine with a cool yet vague expression. She's younger than the rest of us, not more than twenty-two.

"I'm a bit wigged out," she announces, and flops into a chair. Octavia and Andy kiss me, Octavia hands me a gift-wrapped package. "From all of us. Don't bother to open it now. It's Acapulco Gold."

I thank them both, kiss them again, give Octavia her book (*Kama Kala,* lavishly illustrated study of Hindu erotic sculpture) and Andy a picturesque throw-pillow for the house (bright and folksy, with almost psychedelic stripes, made by inhabitants of San Miguel, off the coast of Panama). I tell them to help themselves to a drink, and decide to give Octavia her news first.

"Your father called, from Toronto. Wants you to call Operator four fifty-four, long distance."

"Goddammit." She goes straight to the phone, dials O.

I smile at Rosemary and Andy. "And Mark called. Just half an hour ago."

Gray eyes flicker briefly. "Is he off to the island, I hope?"

"Leaving tonight."

We are all, it seems to me, on islands, Rosemary in her chair, Octavia at the phone, Andy standing near the fireplace, watching me. He looks very like his brother, about an inch shorter; same college-boy smile and open face; hard to locate the difference between them, yet it exists. Imagining a totally horrible situation, in which I can turn only to Jim or Andy, I would choose Andy. It has something to do with his silence, which is not sullen but contented.

"Operator four fifty-four? This is Octavia Fell. You have a call for me from Mr. Skiles in Toronto."

Rosemary gives me a bright, malicious smile. "I'm crazy about your dog."

Andy, still looking at me, asks quietly what Mark said.

"He thinks you're all a bit too complicated."

Rosemary laughs, Andy doesn't. Octavia tells the long-distance operator to hurry it up, please. Getting up, Rosemary admires my dining table. Wants to know where I got it. I tell her there's a store in Beverly Hills that imports furniture from Mexico.

She looks commiserating. "But their prices must be crazy. Bet you paid at least a hundred and fifty for it."

"A hundred and eighty-five, I'm afraid."

"I know a craftsman in Tijuana who'd have done it for thirty." Sits down again. "Don't you hate Christmas? It makes me sick to my stomach." Lights a regular cigarette. "Not even all the commercialization saves it."

"From what, may I ask?"

"From itself. He was born just to make us feel guilty and rotten. I don't think that's anything to celebrate."

"You must feel worse at Easter."

Andy laughs.

"Dad?" Octavia has made contact with Toronto. Rosemary gets up again and stands behind her, putting arms around her neck. "How are you? Merry Christmas. Is it very cold up there?" Octavia's manner is guarded and deferential, quite unlike her. "Thanks for the check. It's really too much. I mean it. You shouldn't. Oh, I'm fine. Oh, very quiet, a quiet kind of Christmas. Warm, though. It's warm and sunny here . . ."

Taking my arm, Andy walks me to the bedroom. He sits on the bed while I stand by the window, gazing out at bamboo jungle, knowing that he watches me, concerned and sympathetic in a maddeningly relaxed way. He wants me to believe that in spite of everything he's a decent person, respects my feelings. Maybe it's true. But he treats me like an outsider. It's like that night at Prell Hall. *We're okay—how are you?*

"So how does it go, Dora?"

I face him as coolly as possible. "Everybody asks me, in so many words, the same thing. But there's a different reason each time. It's Chad wanting me to deal with that dog outside because, if I do, it means I've gotten over Keith. It's Octavia saying I'll be all right if I go to San Diego with her. It's an old lover calling me up to hope I'm okay because *he's* feeling so great, and if I am too, he won't feel bad about having been perfectly foul to me. It's even my hideous neighbor, Mrs. Cody, saying she knows everything's gone wrong, but can't I please behave as if it hasn't. So why do *you* want to know?"

"I just want to know how you're feeling." He smiles. "How you feel affects what you're going to do."

"What do you think I'm likely to do?"

"If you're feeling wrong, I guess you'll do wrong."

"You ask how I am in order to lecture me on how I should be." He takes from his pocket a little box and a pack of cigarette papers. "And if you think _that's_ how I should be, you're wasting your time. I only smoke pot with people I really know and like."

He smiles again and continues preparations.

"Tell me how I should be, Andy."

"I thought you were sick of being told it."

"I am, but I'm curious too."

"Don't you want to sit down?"

"No."

A friendly yet critical look. "You know something? I like you, Dora."

"Everyone else loves me, won't you love me too?"

"I might if you didn't cop out."

"Loathe that expression. It's so smug."

"They dropped you into the world with the same choice as the rest of us. A leaking boat or the ocean." He offered these alternatives with a calm, happy certainty. "Why don't you take the plunge, instead of going down with it and complaining?"

He finished rolling the cigarette and held it out to me. I wanted it. Objected to the mystical act, cure-all carrot dangled in front of donkey, but wanted it. Rosemary, cold and shallow as a bedpan, might have considered herself wigged out; my condition was superconsciously desperate. Also, against my will, I was beginning to appreciate Andy as an antagonist. The more disagreeable I became, the less I ruffled his temper and simplicity.

"If I don't take it, am I copping out again?"

"Right."

"I had a Librium earlier, does it matter?"

"No."

After a series of quick little drags, I passed the reefer back. "Now tell me what you mean by taking the plunge. Turning on and jumping in and out of various beds, up in the hills?"

Although Andy was five years younger than I, his expression suggested a patient uncle dealing with a favorite naughty niece. "That could be part of it. Isn't it good to know more people more deeply?"

"Depending on who the people are."

"They're people you want to know. Then the more sex you have with more people, the deeper you get to know them."

"It may be true in theory but I don't see it happening in practice." More drags. "Octavia was pushing your point yesterday, in her own way. She brought up wife-swapping, which does nothing for suburban couples at all. They remain basically the same."

"Because they're suburban. Leave them out of it."

"All right, what's it done for *you*? Show me your tender perceptions, please. Introduce me to your depth and wisdom."

Andy laughed delightedly. "You're really an arrogant bitch, sometimes."

"Yes, and I think it's getting worse. Partly because what you call knowing people more deeply gave me the most nightmarish evening of my life."

"You have to go back again, and on again, about that night?"

"It was terrible."

"You made it terrible. Keith was right. Nothing made any difference in itself. _You_ made the difference."

"I couldn't help it. Your brother slipped me a hashish cigarette and I wasn't responsible."

"Sure. Everyone was on something, so no one was responsible. If you'd realize that, you'd make more sense."

"Once again, everything's my fault. Octavia says I never learn. Keith tells me I'm unlivable-with. You call me an arrogant bitch. Well, _my_ definition of an arrogant bitch is that bitch in the next room. Rosemary! You can tell at once she's just a beautiful, mean person. Why do you accept her?"

"She accepts us."

"Oh God. We're getting Christlike."

"Is that bad?"

I took a rather feverish drag. "What are we smoking? It feels very strong. Have I been slipped hashish again?" Andy nodded. "You cunning little devil. Funny, that's what I called Jim."

"Stop fighting it. Relax. _Let it happen._"

"How I loathe that expression too. So passive."

"And _making_ it happen is just great?" Andy lay back on the bed, staring contentedly at the ceiling. "_Making_ it happen is the most beautiful thing in the world—making bombs happen, and killings, wiping out leopards, driving turtles crazy?"

"You're sophomoric, the whole pack of you, that's your problem. And who drives turtles crazy, anyway?"

"They exploded a hydrogen bomb near the islands of Galapagos. There's a lot of giant turtles there. They lost their sense of direction and lumbered into the ocean. They

lost their sense of time, thought they were laying eggs
when they were actually dying. I saw it in a movie, _Mondo
Cane_. Know what that means?"

"Yes. It's a dog's world."

For a short time after this I couldn't speak. Tears were
streaming down my face. Andy observed me with a smile
of almost beatific pleasure, which seemed right. I didn't
want sympathy; or, rather, saw that his pleasure was a
form of sympathy, perhaps the highest, much more reassuring than any attempt to cheer me up or ask what was
the matter. He realized my right to weep. He performed a
unique act. He was extraordinary. I wished to tell him so.
Very simply.

"Andrew, you are extraordinary."

He waved a disclaiming hand.

"But you are. You're one of the most extraordinary
people I've ever met. Why didn't I realize that before?"

"You hardly ever spoke to me."

"Right. And I'm not going to speak to you now. I
need silence. Stop talking, please. I'm feeling something."
_He's right about certain things, of course. If you accept
the first thing put in your hand and start smoking it, isn't
it up to you? Why blame anybody? The turtles, although
I identify with them totally, are another problem. In the
meantime——_

My tears had stopped because I was feeling Andy's
smile. It became a kind of X ray, penetrating to my bones,
revealing the smile in my own skeleton. No bitter laugh
or nervous fantasy, this smile was a pure abstracted state,
the surprise of joy. I gave a series of laughs, which Andy
told me afterward sounded idiotic and stupid, the least

likely sounds he could imagine me making; I didn't hear
them, or if I did, had no idea who was making them. A
joke was all I knew, an enormous joke.

Andy shared it, because he began laughing too.

"Oh, you know it too, don't you?"

"Yes, I know it."

"I'm glad. It's such a relief you know it. It's so funny!
It's hysterical."

"No, just funny. Fuck hysterics."

"Right! And fuck hate."

"Right! And fuck war."

"Unnecessary. If you fuck hate, you include war."

"Right."

I gazed out of the window. "And look at that bamboo.
Look at it. It's the jungle."

Arm around my shoulder, he stood beside me. "It's the
outside, Dora."

"Oh, true." I laughed again. "Marvelously funny and
true. The outside is a jungle. Yes. Oh God. And your
sweater is the most beautiful thing I ever saw."

"I agree."

"Stop talking, please. I need silence."

Sat on the bed, aware of Andy watching me, both of
us, it seemed, a little puzzled now. The laughter had gone.
"I promise you, I'm not copping out." Unsure why I said
this; held up my hand, anyway, for him not to answer. A
feeling occurred that it had something to do with my
mother. Image of dead body on beach again. Not agon-
izing this time, but mysterious. "She killed herself, you
know." Couldn't find the connection, yet knew it was
there. Connections always are. I lost the connections in

Bond Street, found them in Venice-on-the-Pacific. Why?
In Venice I wasn't alone. In Bond Street I was all alone,
offered things I didn't want, waiting for my father and
Mrs. Neame to finish their business, waiting to go home
to the smell of an intruder's violets.

"All alone, as I am now." This seemed very bad, and
I didn't like the way Andy was still watching me. In fact,
wasn't sure I liked Andy at all. Cunning, like his brother.
"Come on, Andrew, what's your plan?"

"What?" His smile appeared extremely disingenuous
now.

"You've got a plan. That's why you brought me here. I
can't get out because there's a jungle outside. Jim had a
plan that night, too. All of you did, you wanted to destroy
something in me. But it went wrong, you know, because
I came out stronger. Now what are you trying to destroy
this time? It won't work, but I have to know."

He looked bored. "So we're back to paranoia."

"Oh God, you pathetic creature, is that what you truly
think of me?"

"It's okay. Go on with it and get it over with. I'll sit
it out, though, because it's a bore."

"Thinking people have got plans is paranoia?"

"Right."

"Then I don't have paranoia, because _you_'ve got a
plan!" I saw it clearly now. How careful one had to be.
They were attractive, of course; plausible; experts at in-
ducing false security, knowing I got lost in disconnected
streets and dreamed of deserts, leading me into a luxuriant
maze of permissive so-called love, pretending there is no
other place to go. I almost fell for it, was tempted to

laugh, leave my boat and slide, like those turtles, into the ocean. Seeing Andrew now for what he was, how could I ever have thought him extraordinary? Cunning, like his brother. A kind of evil innocence. They stood side by side, witnesses at my wedding, already planning my grief and humiliation.

"None of us ever makes plans, Dora, so I don't have a plan. But tell me what you think my plan is."

"To get me in bed."

"Can you tell me why?"

"To know me deeper."

He came toward me and said: "You've just given me an idea." He sat beside me on the bed, and pushed me backward. I lay there shouting with laughter—at Malowaka watching us in her feathers from the wall; at the delight of not being alone again; at thinking Octavia must be out of her mind, refusing to find Andy attractive. However, quite soon the bedroom door opened and there she was. Undressing. Rosemary, too.

There had to be a way of dealing with this. After all, it had been easy so far. The way was to concentrate on what mattered, in this case Andy, and forget the rest. *Let it happen.* Then Rosemary, I discovered, had a little tattoo on her left thigh. "Excuse me, don't move for a moment, I've got to see what it says." It said JOE in exquisite blue letters. "That's very sweet and outspoken of you—how is he, by the way?" Realizing I'd misjudged her, I kissed JOE; he proved she had a heart.

The door opened again. Keith wore the black alpaca sweater I'd given him. Skirting a mound of brilliant purple, gold, scarlet and orange clothes on the floor, bamboo forest through the window behind him a living, palpitating, densely green wall, he came over. I pressed his hand to my shoulder.

Nobody, after Keith's arrival, said a word that I can remember; but when the others had withdrawn, leaving us alone in the bed together, I talked a good deal. I'm not sure, I said, whether I've gotten to know anybody any better, but even if I have, it won't mean that I'll be more involved with them. All that occurred was a surprisingly pleasurable exchange. Looking at it in the same light as, say, going to dinner for the first time with people you don't know very well, it presents no unfamiliar problem. If one has a good time, one goes again, or asks them back, and if not, not. Keith remarked that he'd been trying to make this point for months. I know it, I said, but don't you see why I couldn't accept it? The situation has two sides and I was only aware of the other. You may consider it a last vestige of romanticism if I insist that the act of making love can imply a commitment beyond the act itself; all the same, I insist on it. Whatever else one may or may not do, the possibility remains of a special, deeper attachment. In most countries, Keith pointed out, you can only marry one person at a time. Since he married me, what am I trying to say?

Nothing, I answered. I suppose I'm thinking aloud. In fact, I decided to avoid exploring the subject any further, because it would lead into another discussion of our marriage. I longed to ask Keith in what state he now considered it was, but lacked the courage. He wouldn't mention it directly, I knew; the fact that he was here, beside me, in the bed, would have to be enough for the moment.

"Keith, oughtn't you go and see your grandmother?" *Why was I trying to make him go away?* "Thank God she took a nap, but I'm sure she'll be delighted to have you wake her up."

"Okay." He got out of bed at once and started to put on his clothes. I was aware of something oddly docile and indifferent in his manner. Also, the instant he moved away I noticed the room had grown darker. He became a silhouette. I decided to get up too, but found my head foggy and my legs weak. The room looked not only darker but larger, the door an unbelievable distance away.

"Oh God, I can't move."

"Lie down again, then."

"But what about the party? People will be arriving."

"I'll be here."

"You will? I feel terrible about it. After all the fuss, I can't even stand up to greet my guests."

"Don't worry. Take it easy."

"How long do you think it will go on? My condition, I mean, not the party."

"Maybe an hour or two." Keith gave me a quizzical look and moved to the door. Time stretched away now as well as space. An hour felt longer than a year and Keith seemed to be going alarmingly far away. Too late to call him back, he wouldn't hear me. The door closed with a remote echo, as if at the end of a long passage.

Alone in the room, lying on my back, all the bright clothes gone and the bamboo jungle only a vague dark mass outside, I knew I'd been totally abandoned. *Maybe the ocean is cold at first.* When they were all here, I'd kept my eyes closed most of the time, feeling like Orpheus in the underworld. This was compulsive and deliberate. To have opened them would have been like looking back at Eurydice, everything would have frozen, vanished, become lost. I closed my eyes again now, trying to shut out the huge and shadowy room, heard more voices, assumed guests were arriving, and began laughing. *Prell Hall is coming to* me *this time, and how astonished they'll be, paying their mercy call, to find the patient more wigged out than themselves.* Then it didn't seem so funny. Maybe it was what they hoped for; what they'd planned; had I capitulated at last?

Closing my eyes didn't work any longer. I trembled with cold. I was a prisoner lying in a cell. I was a dead body on a beach. They came up and looked at me as I looked at dog. *Who is she? What is it? Who do we call to take her away?*

The phone rang. I picked it up immediately, eagerly, feeling I might be saved by the bell.

"Mrs. Poley?"

"Yes."

A laugh. "You admit it this time?"

"Admit what? Who are you?"

"No one nasty, just Greg."

"Oh God. Excuse me. I was expecting . . . Do you have any news?"

"They got back. And they think it must be theirs."

"I see."

"Theirs is missing, anyway. Was missing before they

went away, but they went away all the same. I wouldn't
do that, would you?"

"No, of course not."

"You better call them."

"I certainly will. No, I'll go round and see them. It's
better."

"Okay. When do I get my dollar?"

"Any time. There's lots of people here, so if I'm out,
I'll leave instructions. You just ask for your dollar and
you'll get it."

"Thanks, Mrs. Poley."

Dog-problem seemed so completely unimportant now,
it had been difficult to concentrate while talking to Greg.
But his call released me from the isolation ward. I was
no longer condemned to this shadowy room while people
arrived, talked, laughed and played music on the other
side of the wall. The world could get through; time ex-
isted again; and I consulted my watch. Almost six o'clock.
That's why the room seemed overcast. The sun had gone
down. Wishing to verify this, I got to my feet, still feeling
unsound but able to walk to the window.

A great night yawned outside. Party sounds drifted
across it on their way to Mrs. Cody. The bamboo wall
looked unnervingly solid and high. Craning my neck, I
managed to see above it, found an acre of clear dark sky
and a single star. This filled me with sudden anguish, it
looked so cold, bright and distant. I remembered the sailboat that I glimpsed yesterday from the coast highway, I
became the wandering bark. The star grew intolerably
bright and cold, and I drifted, it seemed for hours, with
my arms on the sill. A violent spasm in my neck jolted

me back to the room and the party beyond the wall. I was
twisted like a contortionist in order to look up at the sky.

When I faced my party, there were about twenty
people in the living room. I recognized many of them
from that night at Prell Hall, saw Jim himself, of course,
and the dark-haired girl who wore the BRAHMS sweater,
and the other one with the black cape, though she wasn't
wearing it now. Octavia and Rosemary frugged together
in a rather offhand way. Andy came over to ask how I
was feeling.

"I'm all right. Is the party all right?"

He thought it was and asked me to dance.

"Oh God, I hope I can. May we try something quite
slow and old-fashioned, though?"

I glanced through the window as we foxtrotted, saw
two more people coming up the steps. One of them
looked fairly drunk. All the same, he gave dog, hit by the
bluish floodlight, a wide and careful berth. This showed
a certain respect. I was impressed that no one appeared
to have stepped on it or attempted to move it. Somehow
its right to be there had been acknowledged; according
to mood, temperament, eyesight and so on, it became
pop art fixture, happening, sinister ornament, perhaps
even a symbol of the Grim Reaper.

"Who killed herself?"

I stared at Andy.

"You said back there, 'She killed herself, you know.' "

"That was my mother, a long time ago. I was only
six years old. For a long time, it seemed terribly unfair."
He looked puzzled. "What I mean is, I didn't realize what

she'd done at the time. She'd just gone away. When I found out later, it made the world seem a very dangerous place. I felt I should have been warned."

"Does it seem any safer now?"

"No. However, that's got nothing to do with my mother."

Through the window I saw Chad coming up the steps. He carried a long narrow box wrapped in blue and silver paper. I excused myself from Andy and went to greet him.

"Merry Christmas, D.P." Handed me the box, which had a FRAGILE sign pasted on it. "You may hate it, but give it a try, at least."

"Chad! Is it one of yours?"

"The least feminine thing I ever designed, but still quite appealing compared to what you usually wear. Who are all these people?"

"You know some of them. Octavia, and Jim, and Andy."

"Yes." He sounded regretful. "They're all friends of Keith's, I suppose. Who didn't come, I suppose."

"He's here. Talking with his grandmother in the spare room."

"What on earth is going on?"

"I don't know. Chad, may I ask you an enormous favor? The owners of that dog have been away but are back at home now. I ought to go and tell them what happened. I don't want to tear Keith away from his grandmother, but I'd prefer not to go alone."

"A pleasure. Anything, frankly, to get away from this crowd."

"Would you mind very much if we took the dog with us?"

"I don't know. Is it necessary?"

"Well, it belongs to them. They'll have to identify it. Also, I really don't want it around any more, so I'd rather _they_ got rid of it."

"You're much beter, D.P. I suggest we put it in something."

"Gift-wrap it?"

Chad frowned. "That's in bad taste."

"Sorry. I'll find an old bed-sheet."

I told Octavia we'd be back soon and asked her to give Greg his dollar if he came for it.

"But how boring of you, girl, to go off in the middle of your party."

"It won't take long." _What's the matter? She seems hostile._ "I want to get rid of it."

"Why not tell _them_ to come and get it?"

"I find that idea not particularly elegant."

Jim Prell and the dark-haired girl passed by on their way to get drinks. Octavia laid a hand on her arm.

"Elaine, I don't think you ever met your hostess." She introduced us, lips rapaciously parted.

"I remember your sweater," I said pleasantly. "With Brahms on it."

"Really?" She spoke in the same manner. "When was that?"

"Oh, several months ago, up at Jim and Andy's."

"I don't remember seeing you there."

"I didn't have such a sensational sweater."

Elaine smiled and moved away.

"She's a sweet girl," Octavia said.

"Yes, she seems charming."

"You smoked a lot of strong stuff with Andy." Octavia laid a hand on my forehead. "You sure you're all right to go out?"

"I'm fine."

She gave me an amused, doubtful, somehow pitying look.

"I really prefer to get it over with, the way you went straight to the phone, Octavia, for that call from your father."

"He sent me a check. Naturally I wanted to thank him."

She turned away, leaving me to wonder why she apparently resented or despised me now. Perhaps what interested Octavia most of all was giving battle. If there was no promise of a long duel, she lost interest. Our first time at Prell Hall had been excitingly inconclusive; this afternoon, however, I'd been totally willing and compliant but failed to make any declaration afterward. By not telling her that she'd changed my life or begging her to take me to San Diego, I proved my indifference. Rosemary, on the other hand, was ideal quarry. She loved Octavia more than anyone else, yet always threatened to become seriously attached to a man.

I walked down the steps with Chad. Rigid in its blue spotlight, there was no mystery about dog now. It looked supremely irrelevant and pathetic, just another casualty, like the dead rabbit on the country road or the dead gull on the shore. Tijuana Brass music drifted out as Chad shrouded it in a sheet.

"Poor little thing," he said.

"Yes, that's rather how I feel."

Rosemary called out through the window. Laughing, she wanted to know why we were taking it away. Octavia appeared behind her, and said everybody had gotten used to it, they even liked it there. We laid it in the back of my Ghia. I started the engine, switched on lights. Chad got in beside me and switched them off again.

"This may be the only moment we get to talk, D.P. Tell me what's going on."

"I'm truly not sure."

"I suppose I'm speaking out of turn, but you don't belong with Keith, or those people."

"Who do I belong with, then?"

He fitted a long brown cigarette into a holder. "Well, you're basically a solid citizen."

"I deny it."

"It's true. I wouldn't like you if you weren't. What are you laughing at?"

The idea of Chad touting respectability struck me as hilarious. It had its own logic, I could see, for the Fragile customers were basically very respectable women. All the same, tears of laughter poured out of my eyes.

"What is it? Why are you hysterical?" I couldn't answer. "Have you been at the Mary Jane again?"

His choice of this refined expression made me laugh harder. I nodded, then managed to say: "A puff or two, I must confess."

"Are all those people at it?"

"Quite a few of them."

"Then I shan't go back to the party. You might get raided. Nothing's more frustrating than being carted off to jail when you're the only one who's not having fun. And it's very irresponsible of *them* to be doing it all over *your* house."

"I signed that petition, Chad."

"That only makes it more dangerous. They *are* dangerous people!" His burning cigarette waved excitedly in the dark. "They're rootless and egotistical, and it's a mistake to take them on. *You can't win*, D.P."

Glancing up at the window, I had a dog's eye view of the party. I saw Keith come into my living room with Malowaka, his arm around her shoulder. The grandmother walked erect with pride. He introduced her to Octavia, Rosemary, the Prells. They crowded around and soon everyone was laughing. Andy lit her cheroot while she talked her head off. Then Keith went over to the dark-haired girl. They began dancing. I recognized instantly that they would go to bed later.

"I'm not taking anyone on, Chad, I've got a different point of view. If you can't lick 'em, join 'em."

"*Can* you join them?"

"Yes, if it's the only way." Thought of Octavia. "I will *not* give up."

"I've never known your young man particularly well —I'm aware that he doesn't particularly like me—but it's a type I've had considerable experience with, in my own way." Burning cigarette drooped suddenly. I detected a sigh. "It calls all the tunes. It turns all the tables." Aware that I glanced up at my living room window again,

Chad also scanned the scene, saw Keith with the dark-haired girl and kissed me on the cheek. "It is kind only to be cruel."

I said: "But I've never believed in the Schweitzer approach."

"I don't know what that is, or what it has to do with anything."

"It's easier to do what people call good if you cut yourself off, and remove yourself from the main action. Then you can solve nineteenth-century problems in a twentieth-century world. I'm not saying it isn't necessary or valuable, but it doesn't appeal to me. I suppose I could cut myself off now, find a solid citizen I admired and respected but didn't love, and settle for security, but that's nineteenth century too."

Still weak in the knees, I felt strong in the head. I *saw* with an almost disembodied clarity. There were no unquestionable friends, enemies, prospects or fears. There was only the exhilaration of open country and limitless suspense. I started the engine, switched on the lights; heard another sigh from my companion and thought of something else, about which I kept silent too. I could foresee giving up Keith and being consoled by Chad. He would be thoughtful, intelligent, maddeningly right. We would end up laughing and crying together about our broken hearts and the apparent impossibility of happiness. For a woman who was secretly thirty-one (all the disadvantages of youth, impatience and relative lack of experience, without its first flush), a ghastly new role would begin: queen's moll. These are ladies, alarmed by disappointment and rejection, who throw in the towel. They drink too much and have favorite charities. In their late forties they consult a plastic surgeon, who gives them a face lift; everybody tells them how wonderful they look, but nothing happens. Queen's molls are treated with great kindness and have a good time, often more so than with red-blooded gentlemen, but they have thrown in the towel. They are accomplices and victims of charming frustrated queens who unconsciously wish them, for companionship's sake, to remain frustrated. Although concerned to make women look more feminine, and offended by what he considered the transvestism of boots, leather pants, miniskirts and waistcoats, Chad would encourage me to end up metaphorically in drag.

Like a deckhouse on a ship, 138 Palermo Drive projected above a steeply sloping hillside. One parked below and walked up a dark flight of steps, flanked by steamy vegetation. The hill was overgrown with shrubby palms, all kinds of ferns and vines, and the old couple must recently have been watering. A wandering branch brushed against the face, fallen leaves lay underfoot. Things rustled. A few lights from the house showed its large square outline, its flat roof and sweeping bow window on the second floor. Rickety basket chairs were grouped around the front porch. I gritted my teeth and rang the bell, determined that basic indifference to dogs must not show through.

An old man appeared, in shirtsleeves and shorts that bared spindly legs; skin like dark leather, wisps of white hair on his head. He said in a doubtful voice: "Good evening, folks." Then saw the parcel in Chad's arms. "I guess that's it?"

From somewhere above came a loud, querulous female sound. "Who is it? What do they want?"

He turned back into the hall, called upstairs: "It's all right, Nettie. They've brought Phyllis." Asked Chad to leave her on the porch and invited us in. Chad suggested he might care to identify her, and the old man lifted a corner of the sheet. "Yes, that's Phyllis." He started up the narrow stairs, and Chad whispered, "Do we have to?" I felt there were decencies to be observed, and one couldn't simply dump the body and run. Also, there was a strangeness about the house; Chad and I seemed like Hansel and Gretel.

An old woman wearing a blouse and long patchwork skirt sat by the living room fire. Like her husband, she was thin and white-haired, with the same tough, sun-cured skin. The room looked dilapidated; holes and stains in the upholstery, a threadbare carpet, faintly musty smell of ancient plumbing or central heating. But a large moon hung right outside the bow window with its enormous view of canyon, ocean and night, and surf thumped in the distance.

The old man gestured for us to sit down. "Name's Walter Freeman. Wife, Nettie." Heavy Victorian couch uttered a creak. Mrs. Freeman gave us an alert nod and sat waiting. She managed somehow to imply that the situation was more difficult for Chad and me than for themselves.

I lit a cigarette. "Your dog was called Phyllis?"

Mrs. Freeman nodded again.

"I'm so sorry about what happened."

"Wasn't your fault, was it?"

"Phyllis was the roaming kind," Mr. Freeman said. "If you roam, you got to take the consequences."

"Well, I'm glad it hasn't been too much of a shock for you."

Mrs. Freeman smiled thinly. "Expect us to cry?"

"I know how one loves animals."

"Lots of people don't."

"Yes, I suppose that's true too."

"No suppose about it." She sounded querulous again. "It's a fact, Mrs. Poley."

"Nettie doesn't like them," Mr. Freeman explained. "She never wanted Phyllis here in the first place."

"Our son died two years ago." Her tone was matter-of-fact. "He asked us to look after her. Wally and I talked it over and thought it wouldn't be quite right to put her away. But Phyllis never liked it here. Always wandering off."

"Looking for *him*, we used to think," Mr. Freeman said.

"Our daughter asked us over to Granada Hills for Christmas." Mrs. Freeman seemed to impart all events, death or celebration, like a computer. "When we got ready to leave, Phyllis had wandered off again. Drat her, I told Wally, leave a tray of water and a plate of meat in the usual place, and take off. I'm not going to let that obstinate creature spoil our Christmas."

Her husband suddenly rose to his feet. "Afraid we're not very good hosts. Fact is, we seldom have company and we don't drink. Coffee?"

We declined.

He sat down again. "You live in the canyon a long time, Mrs. Poley?"

"About a year."

Mrs. Freeman picked up a long poker and drove it impatiently into a sputtering log, which broke and sank. "We've been here thirty years. You should have seen it then. Quiet. Decent. A good class of people. Now it's packed with riffraff and worse." I thought of 167 Bellavista at this moment. "That's why we seldom go out."

"We don't want to fuss with it," Mr. Freeman said. "We putter around, watch things grow, do the watering."

They exchanged affectionate and contented smiles. Mr. Freeman confided that their golden wedding occurred last month.

"I congratulate you," Chad said. "People don't often go that far. Did you celebrate?"

"We puttered around. There's lots to water and plants like a good soaking. Then Nettie did a cook-out. It was kind of chilly but we wrapped up well."

Mrs. Freeman gave another thin smile. "I'd like to ask you folks something. What do you think about the state of the country?"

"From what point of view?"

"Where's it going? Are we headed for inflation?"

"I honestly don't know. The President seems to think it can be warded off."

"Well, he's paid to think that way. I'll tell you where

I think it's going." She paused. "To the dogs." She paused again. "Take outer space."

"You're against it?"

"Nettie's against fussing around with it," Mr. Freeman said.

"Why spend all that money trying to get somewhere that's nowhere?" Her sharp old eyes fixed me. "No people, no decent air to breathe. It's bad business. They'll never get a return on their investment. As Wally says, let's deal with the Negro race, not the race to the moon."

"And how would you deal with the Negro race?"

My tone must have been guarded and suspicious, for Mrs. Freeman gave her superior thin smile. "Think I'm some kind of extremist? I believe in treating everyone fair, black, white or yellow, if they're fair to me. That's common sense and good business. The kids who take dope and burn their draft cards, that's another thing. They're not fair. If they don't like it over here, I say let them go and live over *there*. You can't drop out so easy, I've heard, over *there*. But the Negroes—take our maid, Bessie. You'll never find a decent more hardworking woman anywhere, black, white or yellow. I'd be happy to have her live next door, if she could afford it."

"Bessie's not the only one," Mr. Freeman said. "They're good people. There's a lot of things they can do."

Mrs. Freeman nodded. "They drive cars, they sing. They preach and wait table. They run the Post Office and trim trees. So why not treat them right? If he said to hell with outer space, I'd put a black president in the White House."

"Our daughter thinks that's going too far."

"Well, Kate's a conservative." Mrs. Freeman gazed sternly at me. "Where do *you* stand, Mrs. Poley?"

"Somewhere between the devil and the deep blue sea, I think."

Mr. Freeman said: "I don't understand what she means."

"She means it's a chancy world, Wally, and she's right."

Chad got up. "It's been nice talking to you. I suppose you know you can call the Humane Society in the morning and they'll come and take Phyllis away?"

"Nice talking to *you*, Mr. Weston." She got up for the first time and I saw how tiny she was, not more than five feet. "I won't let them take Phyllis till I'm sure there's nothing we might use her for."

I stared at the old woman. "What on earth could you have in mind?"

"She might turn into good fertilizer. Plants like that as well as soaking, you know. We'll ask our gardener in the morning."

"He could leave her some place down the bottom of the hill," Mr. Freeman suggested, "where we wouldn't smell anything."

"And Bessie comes tomorrow, too. She might have an idea."

"You're right," Mr. Freeman said. "It's the kind of thing they know."

He showed us down the narrow stairs, shook hands with us on the porch, then glanced at shrouded dog. "Nettie and I certainly appreciate this. There's a lot of folks who wouldn't take the trouble." Leaves and branches rustled as I followed Chad down the steps. By the time we reached the street below, only one light was burning at the top of the house. After fifty years together, more than thirty of them spent on this secluded hill, Mr. and Mrs. Freeman were going to sleep as usual, early and sound.

Beyond my drooping gate, only one light burned too. I saw my living room plainly empty before I noticed all the cars had gone. Stupid with shock, I was shocked again. On the steps where dog had lain, a dark form crouched. After a moment, it rose and moved toward me.

"Oh God. What happened, Greg?"

He shrugged. "You're asking *me*? You told me there was lots of people here and someone would give me a dollar."

"It's true. When you called, I was giving a party." I turned to Chad. "Tell me I was giving a party. This reminds me of a play in which the husband tried to drive his wife mad by hiding things and then making her think she'd lost them."

"Mrs. Poley is telling the truth," Chad said.

"Never said she wasn't. I got here just five minutes ago, saw all the cars driving off, so I figured something must have been going on. Then I figured you wouldn't be too long taking back that dog, so I'd wait here for my dollar."

"I shall make it two, Greg." And did so. "You've done very good work, and I'm sorry you had to hang around to get paid."

"Thanks, Mrs. Poley." He grinned. "Call on me any time." He nodded to Chad and bicycled off down the street.

"I like the way that child takes everything in his stride," I said to Chad. "His home life must be either terrible or wonderful."

"I like the way *you're* taking everything in your stride this time. But I don't understand it."

"Why?"

"You had no right to feel persecuted and almost go to pieces because of that dog. Now you have, and you don't."

Opening my front door, switching on another lamp, I saw first of all a dying fire and party litter, glasses and cardboard plates everywhere, ashtrays heaped with butts, a gnawed turkey leg projecting from beneath my couch. Phonograph still played quietly. Going to turn it off, I found a piece of paper skewered to the turntable stem, revolving with the record. The note was in a handwriting I didn't recognize. *Want to come? Bring passport. South-West Airlines bar.*

Silent, I handed it to Chad.

He said: "Don't. In my opinion, this is too much."

Stared at me. "You won't even *consider* going, will you?"

"Well, someone's invited me. That's progress of a kind. And I'm quite curious to know what it's all about."

Chad supposed dryly that they intended to take a trip: a real one. And it confirmed everything he'd told me earlier. These are not people with whom I belong. It is insulting to treat me like this, unpardonable above all of Keith to leave no word.

"I have to face the fact, Chad, that Keith may not want me to go—or may not even be going." Noticing that

Malowaka's suitcase containing the Broilitzer no longer stood by the door, I checked the spare room at once. The rest of her luggage had also disappeared. "She must be going home, and Keith's going with her. Someone wanted me to know."

"No, D.P. You're invited and asked to bring your passport."

"Oh. That's a point. All the same, her luggage has gone."

"She could be going with them, wherever they're going."

"It doesn't seem likely."

"What does? You're not dealing with people who do likely things."

I returned to the living room and began emptying ashtrays into the fire; added cardboard plates, napkins, and turkey leg; soon there was quite a blaze. I watched it. I threw in dregs of vodka. Flames leaped.

"If anyone wants you to go anywhere, D.P., won't he or she call from the airport? Sit down and wait."

"I don't want to. It's too depressing to go on waiting."

"I'll stay with you."

"I must pack."

Chad followed me into the bedroom. I began putting things in a suitcase: pair of Lady Wrangler jeans, sweater, slacks, dark glasses. Chad grimaced. "At least, dressing the way you do, you don't have the problem of wondering what to dress _for_. But don't you see their behavior is totally and completely unforgivable?"

"It may be. I'm not forgiving anybody yet, I'm just going."

Bathroom: soap, cologne, towels, eye shadow, cold cream.

"You're still under the influence of that stuff, or you wouldn't be doing what you are."

"But it's worn off. I feel unusually clear in the head."

Bedroom again: boots, sneakers, a scarf. _Living room_: passport.

Chad followed me around like a dog that sensed its mistress was going away. "Who are you writing to?"

"The maid. She has a key and can clean up tomorrow. I don't like coming back to a filthy house."

"I'm reassured that you plan to return."

"Can you lend me ten dollars for the maid? I've almost no cash."

Bedroom again: Librium and handful of current bedside reading—Erich Fromm, _The Wisdom of Insecurity_, _Time_ magazine, _The Guinness Book of World Records_. Snapped the suitcase closed. Checked that all doors were locked and began switching off lights.

Chad slumped to the couch. "You're making me nervous, being cool and practical at a time like this." He stared at the ceiling and begged me once again not to go. It distressed him deeply, he said; and I believed him. I wasn't just going away, I was abandoning _him_, wrecking all his hopes for my future as a solid citizen. When I didn't answer, he got up without a word and carried my bag to the car, polite to the last.

Halfway down the steps I paused again, glanced back at the darkened house, imagined a photograph of the scene. It reposes in an album, below the first. _Five hours later_. One sees the silhouette of Dora Poley, beside the silhouette of her tea-plant. In the background, Chad places her bag in the car. This time, lighting does not permit her expression to be recorded, but her posture suggests eagerness rather than alarm.

Freeway, on Christmas night, was fairly empty. I drove fast, enjoying the fantastic illuminated structures of factories and power plants that give Los Angeles after dark the appearance of a science-fiction city, an image of the future. However unromantic the purpose of these buildings (sewage disposal, manufacture of gas), it is disguised by brilliant crosslines, ladders and obelisks of light. Since people have no place in it, the landscape is stimulatingly abstract. It reminded me of a new town I'd seen in Mexico last spring, one of those industrial developments created and set down in the middle of nowhere; extraordinary after driving with Keith through dim, vaguely picturesque villages as much part of the view as cactus and rock. I couldn't remember its name, but the thought of it produced something entirely new. For the first time since I spied, nude and trembling, that dog outside my window, an agreeable episode came back.

Keith had finished a magazine layout of teenage fashions, and suggested immediate departure in his car. In a few hours we'd crossed the Mexican border and were heading into the monotonous northern desert. Before passing the new town, we saw a mountain outlined against the setting sun. It was really bleak, grim and eroded, but looked mysteriously desirable at the edge of dusk. He took my hand; held it; and thought that one day we might build a house on such a place. He had a name for it, *Teonancatl*. This sounded like a volcano to me, but Keith said it was the most secret and ecstatic of mushrooms. Translated, the word meant flesh of God. Eating it, he remarked halfway between a smile and a sigh, was very grave. It was taken only when answers were needed to necessary but dreadful questions.

"Is that your mood right now? You feel it's possible you might want to ask such questions?"

He laughed and shook his head. "Even if I did, I wouldn't ask Teonancatl." Let go my hand. "Would *you*?"

"Possibly. Perhaps. The problem is, how could one be sure of the right answers? An oracle's one thing—at least it's human, or superhuman—but I somehow resent the idea of a piece of fungus having the last word."

Mazatlán, two nights later, was total darkness. There'd been a power failure: pitch-black streets with storm lanterns illuminating a brief huddle of people, forlorn candles glimmering in a few windows, and the ocean like a drop into the abyss. We faced it from the fifth-floor room of our hotel, one candle stuck in a dirty saucer casting huge, exaggerated shadows. Tired from the journey, I was capable only of sleep, but Keith felt restless and decided to go out. I hoped he wouldn't go too far or too long; he wanted only to sit on a bench facing the Pacific for a while. Just before I fell asleep, power was restored and our bedroom sprang into light. In the morning I awoke to find Keith naked beside me, flat on his stomach, face buried in pillow. I read an article in *Life* about the Caucasus, where Russians live to a great age.

Half an hour later he stirred, turned on his back, and

opened his eyes with that familiar uncertain look, surprised to be confronted by myself and the morning.

"Hello."

"Hello." I closed the magazine. "How was it? What
happened?"

"Oh . . ." A yawn. "Nothing."

"Really?"

"I sat on a bench." He stared at the ceiling. "A few
people walked by, nobody spoke. Finally some guy came
up, asked if there was anything I wanted. A waiter at some
restaurant down the street, spoke quite good English. I
said no, but he smiled as if he didn't believe me and
recommended some bar. _El Papagayo_. I asked what kind
of bar and he said it was a good kind. I said I wasn't
interested and he went away. Later I went to find it."

"And how was it?"

"Nothing. Three people and a jukebox. The waiter
was one of the three, he asked again if there was anything I wanted. I said no, finished my drink and came on
back." Pinched my neck. "My adventures are usually
much less exciting than you think."

"I'm glad to hear it. Shall we have some breakfast?"

"Not yet. How long have you been awake?"

"Not long. I read an article about people in the
Caucasus all living to be amazingly old. One man there
claims to be a hundred and forty-five. I wonder why it
happens."

He slipped an arm around my neck. "Doesn't it say?"

"Not really. I suppose it's something to do with being
peasants. They always live longer than townspeople."

"Stop talking about old age. It's depressing."

"I don't think so. I've come to the conclusion I'd rather like to turn a hundred."

His foot gave me a mild kick. "Then go to the Caucasus."

"It's too late. I'm sure you have to be born there."

"You honestly want to live that long?" A stern, quick stare. "What the hell for?"

"It would be an achievement. I'd have to retain all my faculties, of course. It's no good if I'm blind or senile."

"But what's the point?"

"Imagine what one would see. People on the moon. Flying from New York to London so quickly, you arrive before you leave." I smiled. "And computers solving everything, much more agreeably than mushrooms."

"We're very grand and distant this morning. You talk as if everything's other people, and *you* don't exist."

"I suppose occasionally I feel that way."

"So do I, and that's when I think I'd like to die young. We're alike but different."

"How young would you like to die?"

"Forty-six." He frowned. "Maybe, forty-eight."

"That's a cruel age to leave me widowed."

Another kick. "Fifty?" Enjoyed my consternation. "I know you're two years older than you say, I saw it on our marriage license form. Why do you lie about your age?"

"Why do you wait so long to spring it on me?"

"It's not important. I just find it amusing."

In what followed, he seemed to rediscover our first night together, and after considerable ferocity went back to sleep. I got up, had coffee in the empty dining room downstairs to the sound of workmen hammering. Walked outside; explored a few narrow, shuttered streets; recognized signs of disconnection. The modest seaport town was in process of becoming a resort, billboards announcing new hotels, piles of rubble and building materials everywhere. Difficult to be certain what was going up, what coming down. Dogs sniffed at rubbish in the hollow excavated for a swimming pool. A sign promised, HOTEL EL ENCANTO, and inside the skeleton of a first floor an old woman lay motionless on her back, at first sight dead, at second asleep. Flies buzzed around her basket of blotchy oranges and papayas. Church bells rang and a child pissed in the gutter. I wandered along the ocean front, sat on a bench facing the intensely blue Pacific and an island of tall rock, like a ruined castle. The air was like hot breath. From behind, a hand rested on my shoulder. I jumped up in alarm and saw Keith. He carried a copy of the *Los Angeles Times* and showed me a photograph of Mrs. Evangeline Hurst of Cascade, Idaho, attaining her hundredth birthday. She sat by a window and looked out at snow. She said: "It takes faith."

Entering the bar, I heard the strange, rabid whine of a jet taking off; saw, through the window, a lighted plane heading to the sky, then a huddle of bright clothes, purple, tangerine, scarlet and gold, at a table. Six of them, Keith, Malowaka, Octavia, Rosemary, Andy, Jim, with no signs of preparation for travel except for Malowaka's airlines bag on the floor. Before I reached them, a seventh arrived, presumably returning from the ladies' room. Elaine sat down between Keith and Jim.

Keith gave me a nod, friendly but noncommittal. Malowaka said, "I'm glad you made it, honey." Rosemary, reading a magazine, did not look up. Jim and Octavia smiled, Elaine remarked that it had been a nice party. No one showed much enthusiasm or surprise, except Andy, who found me a chair beside him, snapped his fingers at a passing waiter and asked me what I'd like to drink. "Sure am glad you made it," Malowaka said again. "Got to get on my plane in fifteen minutes."

Her plumage, so to speak, looked droopy, and she wasn't talkative. I thought it unnecessary to ask if Keith was going with her, and told her instead I was sorry her visit had been so brief.

"Well, we had a nice lunch together. I liked that lunch." Her tone placed everything, failure as well as hope, in the past.

As I put a cigarette in my mouth, Octavia snapped out her lighter ahead of Andy. "Did you settle your dog business, girl?"

"Yes. It was called Phyllis and belonged to an old couple who seemed strangely indifferent. They care only for each other, I think."

"Good. Bring your passport?"

"Yes." I paused, waiting for information about where everyone planned to go. It was not forthcoming. Instead, Andy touched my arm.

"Look over there, Dora. The table in the corner."

I saw a man probably in his late thirties: classically

handsome, with a straight Greek nose, dark curly hair, broad shoulders. He wore jeans and a thick, shaggy sweater. Opposite him, with his back to me, sat a man dressed in the same way, but with white hair.

Andy said: "That's Mark Cusden. I don't know his friend's name."

Rosemary looked up from her magazine. "Edward." She flicked a page.

"Are we not speaking to them?"

She shrugged. "I'm not. Andy said hello. Octavia went over for a moment and made herself, I'm sure, brilliantly disagreeable."

Octavia raised her arm in a mock-threatening gesture. "I think I like Edward. He's got mystery."

I asked: "What kind?"

The corners of Rosemary's mouth turned down. "Mark."

"Edward used to run a motel in Santa Monica," Octavia said. "One day he sold it and withdrew to the remotest place he could find."

"Nukuhiva?"

"Right. Then Mark left California under some kind of cloud—financial, not moral—and found the same place."

"Stop making it sound trashy," Rosemary said, "like it was written in the stars. I hate the idea of people being destined to meet."

"Why, girl?"

"It takes away free will." She returned to her magazine, impatiently flicking more pages.

153

Elaine, who seldom spoke (to me, at any rate), now did so. "I like the idea of someone taking away my free will. I like just to be _around_—wherever—whatever—you know."

"You like to be no one," Rosemary said, "and you succeed."

"Andy," I said quietly, "please let me in on what's happening. Did _you_ leave me that note?"

He gave me a faint smile. "What note?"

"I see you did. Thank you."

Overhearing, Keith looked across the table at me. I thought of that day at the pool, before we'd even spoken to each other, when he walked toward me with his camera. He seemed to be aiming at me now.

Jim glanced at him, with the same surreptitious smile as his brother. "Do _you_ know what's happening, Keith?"

He shook his head.

Andy offered me a cigarette. "We're going." He sounded deliberately casual. "On a boat. Want to come with?"

"My God. What sort of boat?"

Rosemary laid down her magazine. "It belongs to a friend of mine and it's been tied up in the Marina for weeks. Right after you went off with Chad, I remembered about it. I guess I was loathing Christmas so much I was looking for an escape. So I told Octavia about it and she said, what are we waiting for?"

"But who will drive—steer—this boat?"

"The boys," Octavia said. "Me. You, if you like."

"I couldn't begin, I'm afraid."

"Skippy promised to send me a postcard," Malowaka

said. "Now you're going along too, honey, make sure he does."

Keith was still watching me. "_Are_ you going along?"

"Yes, I believe so." Saw no reaction to this at all. "Do we have any particular destination in mind?"

"Down the coast."

"Mexico? We might put in at Mazatlán."

Keith's eyes flickered briefly. "Did you like it? I didn't find it much of a place." Before I could answer, the loud-speaker announced departure of a flight for Tahiti. Rosemary picked up her magazine. Mark and Edward got up from their table; passing ours, they nodded to Octavia and Andy. I reached out and touched Mark's arm.

His eyes, clear and vivid as a tropical lagoon, had a curious blankness. They looked not through but beyond me. No one, I felt, could block his personal horizon. Close to, he was less formidably handsome; there were saving lines of age, gently puckered mouth, little crows' feet, mixture of sun-bleach and gray in the hair above his temples.

He gave a nervous laugh, that I recognized from the phone. "So our paths cross, after all."

"Yes, they cross and diverge."

"You off on the boat too?"

"It seems so."

"Well, if you find yourself in the South Seas, look us up. We're a thousand miles northeast of Tahiti."

"Straight on past the Disappointment Isles," Edward said, with a look at Rosemary. Even more deeply tanned than Mark, he had the air of a tolerant schoolmaster, amused but watchful.

"Personally, I would adore to, but I doubt we're ready for that kind of a journey. You're not on the phone, I suppose?"

Mark shook his head and laughed again. "We're only just on the map." Another empty gaze from the dreamer's eyes and he went off, Edward following.

They left a silence behind them. I knew that Keith wondered why I spoke to Mark; wondered what game I was playing altogether; probably thought I'd decided to cool it at last. Outwardly, I must have appeared to be in that basically passive state of coolness whose ideal is indifference carried to the point of immobility. Inwardly, I was seething, certain that all kinds of rebellious energetic possibilities lay just below my surface. The problem was, I didn't know what they were. In spite of an entertaining afternoon, remained unconvinced that mass screwing held the key, only that it was preferable to no screwing at all; at the moment, these were the only choices offered. *So then, Dora, watch for signs. Make a first secret resolution to accept rather than reject. Admit Andy is definitely interested, and encourage it. Does the road of excess really lead to the palace of wisdom? All we know is, the road of insufficiency certainly does not.*

Another loudspeaker announcement: Malowaka's plane was ready for boarding. Keith picked up her airlines bag. She got to her feet and made a circle of gallant good-bys, rather like a servant who insists on shaking everyone's hand before she leaves for her next job. She invited everyone to visit her whenever they liked, but not immediately, because the weather would be too cold. Then she asked me to walk with her and Skippy to the gate, stumbled slightly and complained that she felt arthritis returning to her left knee. She slipped one hand under Keith's arm and one under mine.

"If you want," Keith said, "I can still call Silly."

She chuckled and shook her head. "The last thing I need is that face grinning up at me when I hit the ground. I'll surprise him, catch him up to some mischief, most likely. I'll give him hell." She turned to me. "And you're not getting that Broilitzer, honey. There's no point when Skippy says you haven't made up your minds about anything yet."

"You're right. It would be such a domestic gift in the midst of domestic troubles."

"If I understand you, that makes sense. Anyway, it'll be waiting for you if you find you need it."

"Thank you very much, Malowaka. It's always nice to have something to come back to."

She unzipped the airlines bag, took out a plastic bag filled with nuts. "In the meantime, I'm giving you these pecans. We get the cream of the crop." I thanked her again. We reached the gate and she gave Keith a solemn look. "You didn't make it much of a Christmas for me, did you? But since I invited myself, I'll have to forgive you." A fierce, prolonged hug. "I'll tell them all back in Montrose I had the greatest time of my life. That should fix Lucy for a while."

The flight was called again. "Skippy, can I get any Scotch on that plane?" Keith nodded. "Then I'll have a jigger in my coffee. I certainly need something." She kissed me on the cheek. "If you're going along on that trip, don't forget the party spirit." Without looking back at Keith, she walked through the door and her figure disappeared somewhere in the dark field. We saw it again as she moved snappily up the ramp, into the waiting plane.

Lighting a cigarette, Keith continued to stare at the empty field. Finally he said: "I hope it's not the last time I ever see her."

"Why should it be?"

He shrugged. "She's eighty years old."

"That's ridiculous. You feel mildly guilty—which you shouldn't—on account of not going back with her."

"No. Didn't I ever tell you she saved my life?"

I stared at him, then shook my head. He gave me a quick, serious, guarded smile. "It's true. Let's sit down for a moment."

Strangers surrounded us on a leather bench in the boarding area. I felt plagued by their mystery, and couldn't resist the mechanical game of wondering who was going away, who waiting for someone to come back. Noted, while Keith was talking, a passionate reunion (Jewish family) and an indifferent good-by (middle-aged man and wife); was, as usual, fascinated by the people who never moved from their seats at all, reacted to nothing, dozed or stared. Mexican woman with a child asleep in her lap. Pale, elegant girl in a Chanel suit, carrying an umbrella. Two young soldiers who glanced at her from time to time, whispering. A Negress in a purple hat laughing and gossiping with (I think) her sister in orange. All of this, as the final call for Malo-waka's flight came over the loudspeaker, and Keith paused, threatened not to connect.

"My mother got pregnant when she was seventeen. My father didn't want to marry her. He didn't have any money then, either." Keith had left his cigarette on an ashtray at his side; smoke curled up and drifted away. "My mother went to Malowaka and asked for a couple of hundred dollars for an abortion. Malowaka gave her hell. You make that fellow marry you, she said, or _I_ will, and she did, and they lived unhappily ever after." Stubbed out the cigarette. "But I owe my life to her."

"When did you find this out?"

"My mother brought it up, during one of their rows. Weeping fit at the dinner table. I was around fourteen. Next day I went through a cedar chest where my mother kept a lot of stuff—photographs, letters—and found my birth certificate. They'd altered the date on it, to make everything look better or legal or whatever. I asked my mother when I was really born and she said, but it's on the certificate."

A flight to Chicago was announced; Chanel girl with umbrella moved off; soldiers looked disappointed.

"I also asked her about an envelope full of corny dirty postcards I'd found in the chest. She said they were a birthday present from Malowaka, then slapped my face and told me never to pry in her personal possessions again. Anyway, I've never known exactly when I was born. It's not important but it gives you a funny feeling. Also, I'm kind of interested in astrology, and I can't have my horoscope done because I'm not sure when I was born. That's the really frustrating part."

He moved away, began walking back to the bar rather quickly, so that I had to catch up with him. (Noticed, as

I left, that everyone was staring at _us_.) I took his hand, which he resisted for a moment, then accepted.

"Keith, I'd like to ask something, if I may."

"You may."

"Andy asked me to come along, but you didn't. Does that mean you don't want me to?"

"Jesus, have I _said_ I didn't want you to?"

"You expressed absolutely no sentiment either way."

"So what are you after? Of-course-I-want-you-to-come-but-only-if-you-want-to and all that shit?"

"If it's not too much trouble."

"Okay." He stopped, put his hands on my shoulders. "Dora. Sweetheart. I am prepared to state—reluctantly, hesitatingly, but seriously—that I hope you will decide to come." And walked on again.

"Well then, Keith. Hesitatingly but definitely, I will."

When we reached the bar, they were all standing with their bright backs to us, gazing through the window at the airfield, as if drawn to the idea of a departure. They saw Malowaka's plane taxi toward the runway. Unnoticed still, we stood behind them and watched it too.

DECEMBER 26th

AN HOUR AGO, WHICH WAS THREE O'CLOCK in the morning, my watch stopped. Decided not to rewind it, in order to avoid an act of will. Prefer now to stay in a kind of waking dream, consciousness under wraps, emotions allowed the run of the house. This is *not* a vegetable state. Choose deliberately to numb my carping intellect, and thereby embrace more freely anything that occurs. (Otherwise, why be here at all?) All the same, if I sniffed danger in the wings, I would snap out of it; would react; would certainly rewind my watch. Isn't it possible, sleeping beside someone you love, who sleeps too, not to be asleep in regard to that person?

Boat is now a couple of miles off the coast. An hour ago (when my watch stopped), Andy calculated that we'd crossed into the waters of Baja California. One can see nothing, of course. Night is calm and a little foggy; weak moon, in its last quarter, almost lost in the overcast. Wrapped in a blanket, I sit on deck with cigarettes and bottle of wine. A few feet away, totally huddled in another blanket, is something that might be a corpse ready for ocean burial. It is Keith, asleep. The others are "below." Our journey so far is smooth and leisurely; sensation of floating, and of being able to float indefinitely, is agreeable.

Nothing very much has happened yet, except to Rosemary.

Once I ignominiously pretended to know the difference between a cuadrilla and a picador; tonight, openly admitted I couldn't tell a poop from a fo'c'sle. When we boarded, I followed the others down a steep ladder to a very confined space below the deck; with six of us gathered together, it was hardly possible to move. I asked if anyone knew where we were. Keith suggested we might be in the hull, but Jim disagreed, because if so we'd be partially under water. (Relieved to learn this was not the case.) Other suggestions, all betraying frivolous ignorance of nautical terms, were scuttlebutt, winch, crow's nest, futtock, etc. We decided, simply, that we were "below," and this became the word for our wandering cell with its two levels of bunks against the wall, round table fastened to the floor, portable stove and no windows. We could creep through a doorway into pocket-sized bathroom with dwarf john and mini-shower. We could cut ourselves off completely, if we wished, by closing hatch at top of ladder, but Octavia warned we'd asphyxiate by morning.

Prells suggested a joint or two before heading for the open sea. We switched out lights and did them "below," wedged against each other, touching and nudging, listen-

ing to mysterious creaks and faint lap of water. Because
of the darkness, closeness, lack of space, and ground
not quite steady under our feet, it felt like being in a
delicious, secret nowhere. Rosemary, however, became
disturbed. Said the perfume she wore was much too
strong, she didn't see how we could stand it. Our reassur-
ances annoyed her. Equally, she was annoyed that the
perfume itself had cost a great deal of money. "If it was
cheap, you see, I wouldn't care, I'd say to hell with it,
but this is one of the most expensive brands in the world
and they don't realize it's _much too strong_." Elbowed her
way to the bathroom, where she took mini-shower. Odd
thing, of course, was that "below" now reeking with pot,
none of us could smell anything else. When the shower
stopped, we heard a moment of silence and then Rosemary swearing beyond the door. "This is the most terrible thing that ever happened to me! It won't go away!"
Octavia wished to be let in, but Rosemary shouted to keep
out; no one was to come near her, have anything to do
with her, until she'd gotten rid of this dreadful, humiliat-
ing, expensive smell. The door banged open. "Fresh air's
the only answer. I'm going up on deck, so all of you leave
me alone until it's stopped haunting my wrists." She
edged her way back, still swearing, and went up the
ladder.

All of us, I believe, were left feeling like a vacuum
that had to be filled. Andy proposed taking off, which I
seconded. The vote at once became unanimous. While
Jim prepared to start the engine, Andy took the wheel
and Keith stood with one foot on deck and one on land,
ready to untie us from our moorings, Octavia watched

Rosemary ignore everything, leaning over the rail, lolling her arms toward the water, exposing them hopefully to salt and air. She seemed not even to notice when the boat shivered and started to move; ignored the rib of another boat as it passed within a few inches of her face; then sniffed her hands and asked if, when we stopped at the market, we'd bought any lemons. Octavia thought we had, so she hurried back "below" saying: "That should cut it, if anything will."

Elaine wondered whether Rosemary might be going to flip.

"Don't be absurd, girl." Octavia had acquired a yachting cap, which she pushed to the back of her head. "It's just nerves. Rosemary may come on strong, but she's a defenseless child underneath it all. Having suggested this trip, she's just naturally scared." I recognized the shock-treatment approach, crossed my fingers for Rosemary as Octavia climbed down the ladder, and watched, as we moved out of harbor, land becoming a long dark shadow.

Soon it was not even that: a blur, then invisible, with scattered lights above as if suspended in the air. Elaine appeared, having changed into her Brahms sweater. I admitted a tremor at the sight of it, remembering great composer discarded on that bedroom floor in the glow of a burglar lamp. She joined Andy at the wheel. They stood very close together and talked quietly, like conspirators. He put his arm around her. Sipping wine, I knew that my recent friend and lover had decided, for mysterious and arbitrary reasons, to abandon me. It didn't matter, only confirmed yesterday's suspicions of his endearing duplicity. Lured me aboard only to dump me. It seemed suddenly naive.

After casting us off, Keith remained silent. I believed him to be brooding about Malowaka; he curled himself up inside a blanket, position suggesting the embryo she'd saved. The pause seemed necessary and contented. Eventually, I supposed, he could uncurl into life again, with perhaps an uncertain glance at the stars.

A hand appeared and seized my bottle of wine; I looked up to see Jim Prell take a swig. He handed the bottle back, squatted on his knees beside me and gave his dazzlingly friendly smile. At first, neither of us spoke. As usual I'd known he was there but made myself unaware of him; tried now to look at him as if I'd never seen him before, and sighed. Everything too perfect. If only the nose were subtly crooked, or a few freckles broke up the glowing, immaculate tan, or the smile itself didn't suggest he was proud of his teeth—but one was contemplating absolute beauty, and like all absolutes it lacked human appeal. Wine and closeness and night made the moment almost a replica of our meeting at Prell Hall, and since that disaster we'd done little beyond acknowledging each other's presence when we happened to be in the same room. Now, as the saying goes, we happened to be in the same boat. Was something about to begin? If so, neither of us knew what it was. Or _did_ he? Controlling twitch of paranoia as he settled opposite me, against the deck-rail, I summoned a bright attentive look, relieved to find myself unthrilled by disarmingly handsome, innocent face and tall body, unworried by intimations of conspiracy or deceit. It seemed, in fact, that my expectations had never been so calm and objectively inquiring.

From under his heavy seaman's sweater, he took out a little transistor radio. When he switched it on, we could reach only the borderline of various stations, Los Angeles fading out and others not completely fading in. Spanish voice interfered with pop tune, Strauss waltz with newscast, mariachis with revivalist preacher; and ocean slapped against the side of our boat.

He held the machine above his head. "If you just listen to the sounds—not the words or the tunes—what's it like, Dora?"

I smiled at him. "Like everyone trying to get in on the act. Or to many cooks spoiling the broth. Seven's a crowd, you know."

"That's a real knack."

"What?"

"Your way of turning anything into an opportunity to make your own particular point." He sounded pleased. "And your point is never too friendly."

"But you're wrong. It's in simple friendly opposition to yours." Heard and didn't like the hostility in my voice, which made me a liar. Had to admit (to myself only) that I still bore them all a grudge. "Jim, would you please turn that thing off?"

He did so. "You don't like it?"

"Well, I feel more secure when things are relatively clear, or clearcut. That's my simple friendly opposition. All of _you_ get a kind of security out of confusion. I see how it can be done, but I can't do it."

"Now _you're_ wrong. None of us feels secure in confusion. We accept it, is all. It's corny to find confusion confusing."

"Hmmm." More dangerous and interesting than his brother, I began to think. He took another swig of wine and offered the bottle to me, reacting to my disagreeableness with an amused, tolerant superiority, somehow implying that he'd like to like me, but I made it impossible, which was my loss. "I believe in certain basic rules, Jim, because although the time is long past when we have to bother about two and two making four—everything's much too complicated for us to bother about a simple fact like that—we still have to bear in mind that eighty-two and eighty-two adds up to a hundred and sixty-four. Is that clear?"

"Relatively clear. But you said that's enough for you, so feel secure."

"Thank you. I believe I do."

"And what's your point?"

"I still think I made it. You with your cool and reefers and, may I say, group relationships, try to live so that *nothing adds up*. I can't accept that. *Something's* got to add up."

He leaned back, resting his head against the deckrail. "What to?"

"Oh, all the phrases are so shopworn. But let's say, some kind of inner order."

A glance of surprise. "You mean like one thing following another?"

"Yes. But harmoniously! Acceptably! I want, in my life, an acceptable and harmonious arrangement."

"Okay, I'll give you one." He looked at the sky.

"Guide, for Dora Poley, to the inner order of the twentieth century. World War One leads acceptably to World War Two. The zeppelin moves harmoniously to the bomber and the Bomb. The poorer the country, the greater its overpopulation—that's a particularly neat little arrangement, in my opinion. And the inner order of marriage—I'm sure you'll appreciate this one—leads to one hell of a clearcut lousy time." A comfortable stretch and another open, unshadowed smile. "So fuck your inner order, sweetheart. Send it back and demand a refund on your illusions."

He folded his hands behind his head and sat very still. Keith hadn't stirred from fetal position. Like stars in an old-fashioned romantic movie, Elaine leaned in front of Andy at the wheel, his arms around her while he steered. Silence from "below," as there'd been since Octavia followed Rosemary down.

"Hmmm. Then could you possibly tell me whatever it is, or isn't, that you base your own life on?"

"No base. Only a condition."

"I'd like to hear you describe it."

Through a break in the overcast, moon emerged a little stronger. I saw the face of a boy telling his parents he'd met the girl he wanted to marry, heard the voice of someone describing the wonderful time he'd had last night, as Jim explained that for a start, and for an end, he accepted the fact of being completely alone. Around us, the dark smooth stretch of ocean, and above us the same stretch of sky. "I don't want any answers. All I want is release, when I need it." Feeling lonely, or lecherous, he went out to search for whatever might provide satisfaction, always leaving it at that, never pretending it was anything else, never allowing it to become serious, to turn ordinary or ugly or permanent, like love. Feeling depressed by all the other ordinariness and ugliness, of lovers or parents or murderers or nations, he did a joint with people he liked, who were equally happy and alone. Then the troubles, whatever they were, receded into true perspective and he saw their endless insignificance. People and events tried so hard to appear important, and the point, the condition, the security, whatever one called it, was reached by cutting them down to size. "They're not as important as I am, you see." He smiled again. "I've got everything. That's not boasting. It's a fact. I'm more smart and honest than other people. So are Andy, and Rosemary, and Elaine. Octavia could be, but she won't accept another person being less important than herself."

I stared at the pale green wake left by our boat. In the darkness it was like an enormous glowworm. I heard Jim advising me to consider a remark made by Napoleon, one of his favorite historical characters. A brave man, said Napoleon, despises the future. He meant that all anxieties and suffering came from a terrible nervous greed about the future, from wanting to control and assure it. Wasn't I obsessed by the future now, in relation to this trip? If so, remember that a storm could come up any moment and drown us all, thereby making the future totally despicable. Remember, too, that by the time we reached Mazatlán, or wherever we decided to stop, we might all dislike each other so much that we'd abandon ship and return home separately, never to see each other again. Incidentally, he wouldn't care if that happened. It was pleasant, of course, so long as it *didn't* happen; but to care would only bring back all the ugly notions of fear, or jealousy, or loss.

"But suppose, Jim, all that happens is, we make this trip and make it back? Nothing's solved but nothing's dissolved, either."

Wrong again, apparently. There is nothing to solve or dissolve, except in my mind; and it's in my mind, like this wretched concern with the future, because I want to "save" my marriage to Keith. However, there's no marriage to save, only a ceremony performed at my own insistence, a delusion that Keith had obligations toward me because he signed a register. After this encouragement, he offered me a joint, hoping it would put everything— including my marriage—into true insignificant perspective.

"Thank you." Took a drag. "I'll admit that, in one way, I'm more impressed by you than by Andy." Described his brother's lecture on turtles and letting things happen. "At least you, in your own way, *make* things happen—or choose what happens to you. I find it chilling and somehow cruel, but I respect it."

This produced, at last, a flicker of annoyance. "What's cruel about it? Who have I been cruel to?"

"Keith, possibly. I see now that you taught him a good deal."

"If I did, he was perfectly happy till he met you." Amiable again, Jim prodded my leg with his foot. "So I'm not cruel."

I took a series of quick little drags. "Not consciously, perhaps."

"Now that's another real knack."

"What?"

"You're mean about pot, Dora. Did you know that? Everyone comments how mean and selfish you are. You may disapprove of it as a way of life, but let someone pass you a joint and they'll be lucky to see it again."

"It's a more recent knack." Took another drag and handed it back. "I admit I've been greedier about the stuff lately. I seem to have found myself in an increasing number of situations in which it works."

"Is this one of them?"

"Yes." I yawned. "You're beginning to recede into your true perspective. Like that dog, finally."

"But I wonder if it's good for you? Matter of fact, Keith and I thought maybe this trip would be a good time to get you to kick the habit." Smile definitely taunting now; unlike Andy, who became irresistibly kind when I tried to make him furious, Jim offered me a glimpse of delicate steel. "You've got sun and sea air and lots of good canned food, so think about it."

"You are definitely cruel. First you slip me hashish, then you try and make me withdraw."

"First you lie to me, pretend you're an old hand. Then you get a lesson and refuse to learn it."

"But what *is* this lesson? Why am I constantly being told I never learn it, and it's all my fault? And if I find you intolerable, why do you bother to tolerate *me*?" Heard a shrill, truly unpleasant note in my voice this time, and decided not to apologize for it. There was only ocean and night; better to admit, with exhilaration, that I felt myself in the presence of an enemy. "I'd really like

173

to know. You could have persuaded Keith not to let me
come along, and had a much better time."

He didn't answer, only tilted his head against the
deck-rail with an almost dreamy expression.

"Do you have another lesson in mind, perhaps?"

The look, dreamy yet steady, focused directly on my
face. I recognized it. Yesterday, when it came from Andy,
I saw through its false reassuring appeal; yielded to it all
the same, of course, but deliberately—according to my
new rule of accepting rather than rejecting, whenever
possible. This time, however, it was impossible. It was
insolent, superior, and out of the question.

"I'm aware that after a few drags I usually believe
people have a plan, but I've discovered I'm usually right."
Different note in my voice now, coolly experienced, and
false as Jim's expression. "Sometimes I don't know what
the plan is, but this time it's so obvious and unnecessary
that until you give it up I'm not going to look at you."

I looked instead at the greenish wake, which disappeared into nothing, like a broken connection with the
land. Felt another prod on my leg, and continued looking.

"You really think I want to get you in bed?"

"Certain of it."

"Tell me why."

"It's not like Andy's plan, to know me deeper."

"You're damn right. I know you all I need."

"It's destructive. You know I'm here because of Keith,
and if you get me in bed, you make nonsense of why I'm
here and prove your own theory that he's only my delusion."

"Your inner order's confusing you again, Dora. Keith

would feel okay about anything that takes the pressure off himself."

I looked back at him. His expression hadn't changed. I laughed, and he only reacted with a brief, questioning alertness, as if I'd aroused his scientific curiosity.

"But I'm so unimportant," I said, "and you've got everything. I'm not worthy of your lessons."

Putting his arms around me at once, Jim kissed me on an infallible erogenous zone, then asked casually if he was turning me on.

"No."

He kissed me again.

"Well . . . I despise the future." Closed my eyes. "And it's a different kind of thing from Andy. Chilling rather than sweet." Gasped, and heard my voice now like a phonograph record stuck in a groove. "You really are extraordinary, though. One of the most extraordinary people I ever met. Why didn't I realize that before? Stop talking, please. I'm feeling something."

Nothing very much has happened yet, I repeat, except to Rosemary.

When we returned to the deck from "below," Keith hadn't moved. Jim took over from Andy, who said he thought we were entering Baja California waters and went down the ladder with Elaine. I advised them to be as quiet as possible, because Rosemary and Octavia were asleep in each other's arms in a curtained-off bunk. Finding my watch had stopped, I decided not to rewind it, then settled back to blanket, wine, cigarettes, view of night and gathering fog.

Arms outstretched like a ballet dancer's, Rosemary appeared at the top of the ladder and came toward me. "Those lemons worked. But it was nip and tuck for a while, you know." Surprisingly friendly, she sat down at my side and jerked her thumb in the direction of Keith.

She said: "It likes to sleep, doesn't it?"

"Yes, it does."

"Isn't that rather a bore? Spending so much time, I mean, waiting for it to wake up?"

"Yes, a bit."

"Still, you do love it very much. Don't you?"

"I'm afraid so."

"Wish you didn't?"

"Occasionally. At the moment it doesn't matter, because I've just been to bed with Jim."

"I thought you seemed kind of relaxed. But let's get back to the main subject. Why do you love it so much?"

"You know one can never really answer questions like that."

"But you try. All that trash you gave Malowaka about driving across America and getting a thing about it."

I stared at her. "She told you? The old buzzard actually repeated what I said to her?"

"She told us all, at the party, right after you left to take back that dog. She didn't really understand what you meant, but it kind of impressed her, and she said, 'Skippy, that girl has got very interesting and peculiar reasons why she loves you, you ought to ask her some time.'" _That must have been the moment when, sitting in the car with Chad, I glanced up at the window and saw him begin to_ *dance with Elaine*. "Frankly, and I'm not bitching, I don't think you love him at all. You're just hung up."

"Well, Rosemary, I've never been quite sure what being hung up means, except it's no good."

"It's when a person isn't what you expect and becomes a problem. You try to solve the problem even though the problem only exists because the person isn't what you expect. I hope that makes sense and I honestly hope you solve the problem, because I like you. I didn't at first, but when you kissed ᴊoᴇ and asked how he was," she leaned her head against my shoulder for an instant, "I was completely yours."

"I'm glad. I know I can be forbidding, especially when I'm unhappy, but I really do prefer to be friends. Do you love Octavia, by the way?"

"No, but she'd follow me to the ends of the earth. She's got this terrific thing about me, and I'm impressed, and I can't ignore it. Besides, I like to be followed." An inkling of regret—the most, probably, that she would ever allow—could be detected in Rosemary's voice. "I'd rather be followed by Mark, of course. But he won't. So what are you going to do?"

"I can only hope, somehow, it turns out all right."

"Well, I'm lucky." She laughed. "In the end, I honestly don't care one way or the other."

"How I envy you."

"Why? Being followed by Octavia is hard work."

"I meant, not caring." Looked at the wake again, wriggly and mysterious in the drifting fog, a question mark extending nowhere. "Why can't I make that scene, I wonder? What is the difference between me and everyone else on this boat? Why do people let me in and then try to kick me out? Why are all those beautiful men so strange and frustrated? Rosemary! *What is the matter with everything?*"

She smiled. She squeezed my arm. She looked at me with her veiled, lovely gray eyes. "All sensitive people get depressed at Christmas. There's this terrible pressure to feel awful, because of *Him*. You just have to sit it out, get drunk, or stoned, or laid, or followed." She stood up, stretching her arms again. "But look where we are! It's so beautiful being where we are. I was ready to die at first, when I realized I'd landed myself in a place where Octavia could *really* catch me if she followed me—because I couldn't get off, you see—but then I thought, that's ridiculous. When I finally *do* get off, I'll feel wonderful." Contented sigh. "If you really work things out, Dora, all the way, you'll always be free. So how can you seriously think anything's the matter with anything?"

This dawn was roused from nap by sudden cry of gulls. Eyelids blinked open as they circled above, barely outlined against the gray of mist. Couldn't remember for a moment where I was; then saw Keith still curled in his blanket; and Octavia at the wheel, like the Flying Dutchman in her yachting cap; and remembered that I, Dora Poley, was nowhere at all. Bones damp and creaky from the night on deck, I reached for wine and found my bottle empty. Heavy-eyed, I peered for a sign of land, but wherever it was, near or far, the fog shrouded it. Limbs aching, I rose to my feet, and *The Guinness Book of World Records* dropped from my lap to the deck. It seemed unlikely this

little volume could offer much help or consolation—
would have preferred _Information Please_—but I picked it
up, clutching at a straw, flicked through pages and discovered I was afloat on the largest ocean in the world,
covering about one third of the entire surface of the earth,
with an average depth of 14,048 feet. If you followed a
particular course on this ocean, I read, you could reach
the world's most distant point from land. Glancing at
Octavia, I hoped her pilot's hand was firm.

"My poor angel." She met my glance. "How do you feel
this morning?"

I went over. "Undecided."

"I was afraid of that. You were sitting there looking
at Keith exactly the way you stared at that dog."

"Not really. I was just wondering whether or not to
wake him up."

"Why not let him sleep?"

"I want to talk to him."

"It can wait."

"How do you know?"

"You've nothing important left to say to him. Light
me a cigarette instead."

When I did so, she said: "Put it in my mouth."

I did this too, and she pulled me toward her, as Andy
had done with Elaine. I leaned against her while she
steered. Wisps of fog blew across. It was damp and a
little chilly, and being with Octavia felt pleasantly warm.
I liked the idea of her as pilot, too.

"Of course, I realize that wanting to wake Keith up
has a certain symbolic meaning."

"Then forget it."

"Why?"

"He won't like being waked up in the first place, and if you tell him the reason's symbolic, you'll make him really angry."

"I suppose you're right."

"You bet I am." Her arms tightened around me. "Right for you, Dora."

"You must stop that or I shall have to leave."

She stopped. From the direction of land, low in the sky, I saw a faint and discouraging yellow blur. Sun was rising behind heavy overcast. The trip had aroused hopes of tropical warmth. So far, I had lived through a foggy night; Jim Prell explaining to me about life, and how he was the most important person in it, and almost making me believe him for about half an hour; and a motionless, silent, sleeping Keith.

"Octavia, I have the impression he's sleeping off quite a few things. Malowaka. Christmas. A year of marriage to me."

"There you go again. Just let him sleep."

"All right. And if, by the time we get to Mazatlán, nothing at all has been settled, I shall leave. I shall go off somewhere by myself. I have a passport and, mortgaged to the hilt though it may be because of buying that home for Keith, a decent private income."

"If you do, get some directions from Andy first. He knows the country well."

"He'd only direct me to some mushroom fields."

"You could do worse. And if you did go off, you know, I might follow you."

"Octavia, I really adore you."

Mistakenly encouraged, she tightened her arms around me again. "I know."

"Because you're not afraid of being absurd."

Leaving her, I went back to Keith. The form beneath the blanket was, like the sun, a discouraging blur. Octavia was probably right. If I woke it, would anything become clearer?

After a moment, I called his name. Loudly. First response was an oath from Octavia, and the boat threatened to change direction for a moment. I glanced up and saw her immersed in disapproval, fist on hip, cap pushed further back on her head. Then, with a shrug, she steadied the wheel.

The blanket stirred. It uncurled, and became upright. Through a grudging slit, a pair of Indian eyes fixed me with a frown. After a while, they mirrored a series of familiar questions: who is this person, where am I, is it really another day? The questions were answered, and he sighed.

"What is it, Dora?"

"Nothing."

"You woke me up."

"Yes."

"Then what is it?"

"Nothing. I've had, for several hours, a desire to wake you. I've resisted it until this moment. Now, in spite of Octavia's warning, I've given in."

"You always lie."

"No. When I called your name, I had absolutely no idea what I was going to say next. Like the day before yesterday, when I drove up to Prell Hall to see you, with-

out really knowing why. However, now I've woken you,
I admit I've got a suggestion to make."

"Give me a cigarette first."

I did so, then lit one for myself. Smoke issued from the
slit in the blanket, while the eyes continued to watch me
with suspicion.

"Let's bullshit, Keith."

He had a mild coughing fit, spat on the deck, and
apologized.

"I want to bullshit with you," I said. "I never have.
It's one of your great pleasures that for foolish reasons I've
never tried to share. Now I'm ready."

"Are you stoned?"

"Not at all. Took my last drag hours ago."

"Who with?"

"Jim Prell."

"Ah!" The slit widened. "And how was that?"

"Interesting. For the first time, we seemed to get
through to each other. As a result, this morning, I'd like
to ask permission to join the whatever-happens-happens
circuit."

"Did whatever-happens-happens happen with Jim?"

"Well, yes, it did."

Keith smiled. "So you woke me up to tell me you and
Jim made it last night. Thanks, Dora. You're the greatest.
I'll go back to sleep now."

He withdrew into the blanket, closing the slit. Sudden
contortions occurred within. Having forgotten about his
cigarette, he reappeared hastily, threw it out, and withdrew
again.

"That wasn't my reason, Keith. We're just bullshitting,
aren't we? Jim's name came up, and it led to something

about the two of us, but it's not important. I'm just sitting here, looking at the ocean—next best thing to your grandmother's mountains—and wondering whether I really wanted it to happen, and, therefore, if it did."

After a moment, he opened the slit again. A pair of dark glasses confronted me now. I laughed and said he reminded me of an Arab woman. "Haven't you seen them, Keith, in those shapeless garments—haiks, I think they're called—with sunglasses propped in front of their veils?"

"Are you still wondering?" No smile in his voice. "Or have you reached a conclusion?"

"I don't think I will. Conclusions are too definite. Too committing. The only one I might reach is that I don't care whether it happened or not."

"You're lying again."

"No, just bullshitting. But if I'm not doing it right, you must correct me. As a bullshitter, you see, I'm a virgin. By the way, isn't it disappointing about the weather? Do you think we're ever going to see the sun?"

"You're forcing it. I know it's difficult for you, but try and relax."

"I'm sorry. Jim said something very basic about himself last night. He feels basically alone and likes it that way. What about you, Keith? Do you feel the same?"

He removed the dark glasses, demanded another cigarette. I gave it to him. "Yes, I feel the same," he said. "But not because I like it. I can't help it."

"Why?"

"Too many defenses."

"Are they unbreakable?"

A shrug. "You should know. No one's tried harder to break them."

"But I don't know. I only believe that, secretly, you find something romantic in your situation."

"Bullshit."

"Exactly. Your supreme bullshit. You imply that your situation makes you suffer, but the drama of it appeals to you."

Unexpectedly, he laughed. "Depressing, isn't it? I mean, all that stuff about wanting to communicate and being unable to—it's so out of date."

"I must say I agree. Smiles are in, Keith, and sulks are out."

"So what are you going to do?"

Because I didn't know, I didn't answer. Instead, I asked Keith if he had a pencil and paper. He produced them from inside the blanket. I stared at the blank sheet of paper. _Order pad swinging from chain around a uniformed waist. Can I help you?_ I wrote: "Hello! My name is Dora," folded the paper and slipped it inside the empty wine bottle. I corked the bottle and threw it over the side.

"What did you write, Dora?"

"I'd rather not tell you the exact phrase. But it was a kind of open invitation to everybody. I made it clear that I'm _here_—wherever that is—in the world, on the market, and all the rest." Saw the wine bottle bobbing on the grayish ocean. "There I am. On my way."

He looked curious but disconcerted. "What made you do that?"

"Just bullshitting."

"I don't get your mood. It's a new one."

"It's cool."

"I'd like to believe you."

"Please do. You see, I can't yet visualize a time when I

won't love you, or when loving you will make me happy.
In the same way, you don't want to let me go, not because
you can't live without me—when the chips are down,
you can live without anybody—but you don't want the
personal failure of losing me. So neither of us can break
out of our situation, and it makes no difference at all what
we do."

"But you make us sound just like other people." Smiling faintly, he reached out to touch my hand. "Don't
forget to send Malowaka a postcard if we get anywhere."
Put on dark glasses again and continued to sit, impenetrable, blanketed in solitude.

Jim, Andy, Rosemary and Elaine came blearily up the
ladder, yawned their way to the side, leaned over and
gazed at the ocean. No one, as if an agreement had pre-
viously been made, said good morning to anyone. Since
no one truly cared about anyone, it seemed appropriate.
_Very well. If you can't lick 'em, join 'em. Three mornings
ago a screech of brakes brought you out of a dream, and
you found a dog blocking your view. How's your view
today? Well, it's different. You're not just looking at the
ocean, you're on it. And there are four people with their
backs to you, peering into it; and Octavia, at her misty
helm, steering you through it; and a pair of dark glasses
looking out from a blanket. Oddly enough, all of this
connects._

There was something else, too, which I'd forgotten
about for a moment. But a moment was too long. When
I moved to the side to look for my wine-bottle floating on
the waves, I couldn't see it anywhere. A little shock of
disappointment, then I didn't care at all. Could launch
another one later, depending on events.

About the Author

GAVIN LAMBERT was born in Sussex, England, in 1924. A graduate of Oxford, he took up film work in London and was film critic and editor of *Sight and Sound* from 1950 to 1955. He has lived in California since 1957, became an American citizen in 1964, and has written numerous movie scripts, including "Sons and Lovers," for which he won an Oscar nomination, "The Roman Spring of Mrs. Stone," and "Inside Daisy Clover," adapted from his novel. Other books include *The Slide Area,* a collection of stories about Hollywood, and *Norman's Letter,* which won the 1966 Thomas R. Coward Award in Fiction.